The Sins of Motherlode

Sin was a profitable commodity in a mining town like Motherlode. Lust made money for the madam, wrath and avarice created targets for the manhunter, and the newspaperman was greedy for stories.

'He had no right to take you against your will.' When a prostitute is raped during the robbery of the Motherlode stage, Jonah Durrell seems to be the only man who cares. The handsome manhunter can never resist a damsel in distress. He is determined to get justice for Miss Jenny's girl, and recruits Robinson, an enthusiastic newspaperman who witnessed the attack. The women are not meek and passive though. They are willing to take matters, and guns, into their own hands to survive in a tough world. Together, with Durrell and Robinson, they begin to uncover the layers of lust, avarice and envy in town, bringing down the wrath of their enemies. Can the women of sin get the justice they deserve?

The Sins of Motherlode

Gillian F. Taylor

A Black Horse Western

ROBERT HALE

© Gillian F. Taylor 2018
First published in Great Britain 2018

ISBN 978-0-7198-2701-3

The Crowood Press
The Stable Block
Crowood Lane
Ramsbury
Marlborough
Wiltshire SN8 2HR

www.bhwesterns.com

Robert Hale is an imprint
of The Crowood Press

The right of Gillian F. Taylor to be identified as
author of this work has been asserted by her
in accordance with the Copyright, Designs and
Patents Act 1988

Typeset by
Derek Doyle & Associates, Shaw Heath
Printed and bound in Great Britain by
CPI Group (UK) Ltd, Croydon, CR0 4YY

CHAPTER ONE

'I do beg your pardon, yeah?' The tall man drew his gangly legs in sharply after inadvertently bumping them against the skirts of the woman sitting opposite him in the stagecoach. Although nearly thirty, his long limbs gave him a coltish look. Curls of thick, brown hair were escaping the control of his patent hair oil and his bony face was unsuccessfully decorated with the latest style in side-whiskers, but he had a winning smile.

'Thank you,' the young woman replied quietly. She was a green-eyed redhead, her hair worn in a coiled braid on the back of her head.

The man raised his broad-brimmed hat to her. 'Hulton F. Robinson at your service, ma'am.'

'Miss . . . Waterford,' she replied.

Robinson noticed a very slight hesitation before she spoke her surname, but before he could form a polite question, one of the other three male passengers spoke up.

'Hulton F. Robinson? I seem to recall seeing that name in a newspaper.'

Robinson smiled proudly. 'I'm a correspondent for the *New-York Tribune*, and the *Rhode Island Chronicle*,' he added.

The other man nodded. 'The *Chronicle*, I used to read that sometimes, back at home, 'fore I come along of Colorado.'

Robinson's smile sagged briefly. It was wonderful to have his name recognized, but the local paper from his hometown hardly compared to the prestige of the mighty *New-York Tribune*. A few moments later, his natural optimism had reasserted itself, and he was digging in his jacket pocket for the notebook and pencil that accompanied him everywhere.

'May I ask, what brings you to Colorado, Mister. . . ?'

'Hopgood. Well, sir, I'm a carpenter. . . .'

Within a couple of minutes, Robinson had got the names and businesses of the other three men on the coach and the second female passenger. His pencil flickered across his notepad, producing a shorthand that was surprisingly neat, given the rocking of the coach on the dirt trail. The pencil jerked across the page when a couple of shots cracked out from somewhere nearby. As the passengers looked up, they heard a shout, demanding the coach to halt.

'Bandits!' exclaimed Hopgood, as the regular pounding of the team's hoofs broke up and the stage began lurching to a sudden halt.

Robinson used his long legs to brace himself as he dropped notepad and pencil into his jacket pocket. He quickly whipped out a wad of notes from his wallet, and tucked them into the crack between the seat and the side of the stage. He was done just before the stage pulled up. Bandits were at the side of the stage almost immediately. The doors were yanked open and men wearing bandannas tied over their faces, gestured with guns.

'Everyone out this side, pronto.'

Robinson was nearest the door. He folded his ungainly height through carefully, then turned to give Miss Waterford a hand down the step. The other passengers followed and soon all six were lined up near the coach. Steep mountainsides rose either side of the tumbling River Animas as it wound along the flat floor of the valley. Masses of dark green pines scented the clear air, with the bright splash of yellow aspens clustered here and there on the lower slopes. No one was looking at the lovely scenery though. By turning his head slightly, Robinson could see a bearded man covering the stagecoach driver and guard with his pistol, while two other bandits lowered a chest from its place beneath the driver's seat on the front of the stage. He kept more of his attention on the men

7

who were holding the passengers at gunpoint.

They were the two who had opened the doors; one had come around the back of the coach to join the first. He now pulled a small, cloth bag from the pocket of his brown jacket, and shook it out. Holstering his gun, he approached Robinson cautiously.

'Don't any of you make any fuss now,' he warned, his voice slightly muffled by the stained bandanna over his lower face. 'My buddy's watching you. We just want your valuables.'

With his right hand, he cautiously patted Robinson's clothes. He found the newspaperman's wallet and plain silver pocket-watch. The watch was returned to Robinson's pocket, but the wallet was opened and the few dollars inside removed and dropped into the cloth bag. The bandit moved on to Miss Waterford. He took money from the reticule in the pocket of her skirt, then reached for the gold bar brooch at her throat. Miss Waterford stiffened, but stifled the protest she'd been about to make. She stood still, her lovely face expertly schooled into stillness as the bandit unfastened the brooch and yanked it free.

'Pretty thing,' the bandit muttered, glancing from the brooch to the woman. He paused and stared intently into her face, then took a step back and looked her up and down. 'Well, I'll be damned.' He turned to the bearded bandit who was covering the driver and guard. 'Hey, boss! This here's one of the doves from that fancy parlour house in Motherlode. I wanna see if she's as good as they reckon.'

'You sure?' the leader called back. 'Remember, we don't hurt women.'

'You bet I'm sure. I saw her out with that tall madam and there ain't no decent woman would be seen talking to her. 'Sides, you can't mistake that red hair.'

The leader glanced at the chest and the two bandits who were transferring its contents of moneybags to the pack saddles of a couple of mules. 'Get the other passengers' money, then be quick with her,' he ordered. 'You'll take extra watches,' he added.

The bandit hastily relieved the other male passengers of their money, and a gold watch belonging to Gibson, the businessman. Dropping the cloth bag near the man holding a gun on the passengers, the bandit grabbed Miss Waterford's wrist.

'You're mistaken,' she pleaded as he pulled her out of line.

'Please leave her, yeah?' Robinson added impulsively.

The bandit continued pulling Miss Waterford away. 'You're a whore an' you know it,' he said. 'She's just doing her job, 'cept she ain't getting paid this time,' he added generally.

Robinson clenched his fists in frustration, but the bandit watching them was tensely alert, his Colt aimed steadily at the male passengers. He took a quick glance at his companions, but none of them were armed and all the bandits were. Miss Waterford was pulled away to a spot near the trees, but still in plain view of the coach, and thrown to the ground. She made no protest or attempt to struggle as her skirts were roughly pulled up. Robinson looked away as the rapist held her arms with one hand and began fumbling at his belt with the other. He glanced at the other woman passenger, Mrs. Thompson, who had her eyes closed and looked as though she wanted to cover her ears. There was nothing he could do to help anyone now, so he concentrated on the man holding them at gunpoint, trying to memorize as much as he could about him.

As he stared, Robinson could hear the muffled chink of the moneybags being moved, the gentle sound of the river, and the steady grunting of the bandit forcing himself on Miss Waterford. A quick glance revealed that she was lying still with her face turned away.

'Hurry up,' called the leader. 'We're nearly done with the money.'

Two minutes later and the worst was over. Miss Waterford was pushed back to join the other passengers. She kept her face averted from them as best she could. Her cheeks were flushed and Robinson could see a smudge of tears on her eyelashes, but her expression gave away little. The businessman, Gibson, helped Mrs. Thompson back into the stagecoach, making sympathetic noises about her ordeal as she sniffed and dabbed her eyes with a handkerchief. The other two men followed, leaving Robinson and Miss Waterford standing together.

She looked at him and waited, expecting him to ignore her. Something in her quiet dignity moved Robinson to take her hand and help her aboard. Her face warmed at his gesture, and she murmured thanks as she climbed inside. Mrs. Thompson rather obviously drew her skirts aside as Miss Louise took her place opposite, but otherwise ignored the other woman.

As they settled themselves, they heard the leader giving instructions to the driver.

'You can see my pal there on his horse. He's gonna cover you for fifteen minutes while the rest of us get away. You try making any move afore then, and he's gonna start shooting. Just you all wait nice an' peaceful, and won't no-one get hurt.'

A group of hoofs moved away, but the stagecoach remained stationary. Gibson, the businessman, grumbled and finally announced he was going to sue the stage line.

'Don't the tickets say something about travelling

at your own risk, yeah?' Robinson enquired. 'And anyway, I reckon Miss Waterford's got a better claim for damages than you.'

'If she's a whore, then her goods are soiled anyway,' Gibson returned.

There was a sob, but no other sound from Miss Waterford, who was staring out of the window towards the river. The passengers fell silent again. After a few moments, Robinson took out his note-book and began to write.

There could hardly be more contrast in appear-ance between the two men riding together along the main street of Motherlode on that same fall afternoon. The man slightly in front, on a fine dapple-grey, would be an eye-catcher in any company. He was tall and athletically built, with black hair and dark eyes. A small scar on his right cheekbone only added a roguish touch to his unusually good looks. He had the gift of being able to wear any clothes well, and showed off the well-made black jacket and trousers and the red and gold embroidered waistcoat over his white shirt, beautifully. The smart, well turned out appearance tended to distract people from noticing the two fancy matched Smith and Wessons he wore in a tooled leather gunbelt.

Slumped in the saddle of a nondescript bay, a length behind, was a lumpy, unshaven man in hard-worn trail clothes. The mousey-brown hair showing under his scruffy hat was in need of a trim, and even the fact that his hands were cuffed together failed to draw attention from the man ahead, who was leading the prisoner's horse.

'This is our stop,' said the handsome man cheerfully, turning his grey towards the hitching pole out front of the marshal's office. Dismounting gracefully, he hitched first his own horse, and then the bay to the pole. Approaching his prisoner from the bay's off-side, he warned, 'Don't make any fool moves now, Brown.'

'I know you, Durrell,' Brown replied.

Jonah Durrell unlocked the handcuffs and stepped back, the metal cuffs dangling carelessly from his left hand as he watched his prisoner. Brown kicked his feet free of the stirrups and leaned backward in his saddle, stretching his arms out to each side.

'Man, that feels good,' he exclaimed, circling his shoulders to loosen them.

With no other warning, he swung his left leg over his horse's neck and jumped down, using his momentum to swing a powerful blow with his left hand.

Jonah simply took half a step back, out of range. As Brown's fist harmlessly passed his face, Jonah stepped forward again and drove a short punch into Brown's jaw. Brown staggered back, bouncing against the side of his horse, which snorted in alarm. Gathering himself, Brown lunged forward, feinting with his left hand while following with a hard right. Jonah stepped nimbly to his left while bringing up his right arm. Brown's feint hit only air, throwing him off-balance slightly as Jonah deflected the right-hand punch with his right arm. He pushed the outstretched arm hard enough to twist the unsteady man around. As Brown staggered, Jonah took a fast step after him and slashed the metal handcuffs across the back of his head.

Brown stumbled forward, half-catching himself on the hitching rail. As he tried to pull himself back up, Jonah pursued him. Grabbing the collar of Brown's jacket, Jonah pulled him away from the pole then abruptly smashed his head back against the wood. Brown let out a grunting groan and subsided to the edge of the rubbish-strewn sidewalk. As he collapsed, the door of the office opened and the marshal himself came out, shotgun in hand.

'What the hell . . . oh, it's you,' he finished, looking first at Jonah, and then at the man slumped against the wooden boards.

'Good afternoon, Marshal Tapton,' Jonah said cheerfully, quite unruffled by the short fight. 'This is Pete Brown, wanted for armed robbery in Animas Forks.'

Marshal Tapton grunted. 'Bring him in then.'

Jonah Durrell efficiently cuffed his prisoner

again, hauled the man to his feet and pulled him round the horses and towards the marshal's office. As he crossed the sidewalk, he gave a dazzling smile to a weather-beaten woman in hard-worn, modest clothes who was holding a laden basket of freshly cleaned and ironed clothes of better quality than her own. Her eyes widened at Jonah and she automatically smiled back, colouring prettily at his attention. Jonah was cheerful as he entered the warm office, knowing that the washerwoman would treasure the memory of his smile at her. He was vain of his good looks, without taking his vanity seriously, and had real pleasure in using them to brighten other people's lives, if only for a few minutes.

Although it was a pleasant September after-noon, the coal heater in the marshal's office radiated enough heat to make the place slightly too warm for most people. Tapton was a work-toughened man, starting to spread at the waist as middle-age set in. His craggy face was decorated with a flourishing moustache and side whiskers, intended to draw attention from his impressive nose. He had already opened the door separating his office from the cells at the back, and Jonah led his grumbling prisoner straight through. Taking Brown into the cell Tapton had opened, Jonah removed his handcuffs and retreated.

'You saw him beat me up,' Brown called to the

Marshal as the door was locked.

Tapton just looked at Jonah.

'I warned him, but he was fool enough to try jumping me when I let him off his horse,' Jonah commented. He had a clipped, New England accent that suggested a good education.

'You're plumb lucky he didn't shoot you,' the marshal said unsympathetically to Brown. 'Son-of-a-bitch is as smart with them guns as he is with his fists.'

Jonah smiled at the mixture of compliment and insult, and followed the marshal back into the too-warm office.

Handing the marshal a wanted notice he'd pulled from his pocket, Jonah waited patiently as Tapton carefully scanned the paper.

'A hundred and fifty dollars for Brown,' the marshal muttered. 'I guess that's him you brought in.' He looked at the manhunter. 'It's a dirty job you do, but you do it straight.'

'Where there's mines, there's robbery, gambling and drinking. You get folks as crooked as a barrel of fish hooks, and some just plain drunk and mean, and the county sheriff can't keep on top of it all,' Jonah answered, as the marshal began opening his safe.

'Someone's got to take care of the folks in town, and someone's got to go chase the wrongdoers hiding out in the country,' Tapton answered with a dry snort. Getting some paper from a drawer, he changed the subject. 'You got some doctor training back east, didn't you? Whyn't you finish your studies and set up practice out west? Folks need doctors more'n they need manhunters.'

'With the way the new country is at the moment, I'd say there's room for both,' Jonah answered, as the marshal began writing out a receipt. 'I turn my hand to medical work when someone's in need of it, but manhunting pays better,' he said honestly. 'I can do medicine full time when I feel I'm not quick enough to go on with the manhunting.'

'If the manhunting don't kill or cripple you first,' Tapton responded, pushing the receipt and pen across the desk.

Jonah glanced over the receipt, dipped the pen in the inkpot and signed his name with a flourish. He was putting the cash in his billfold when a flurry of noise and activity in the street outside drew both men's attention to the window.

'That's the stage from Silverton,' Tapton exclaimed. He glanced at the clock ticking on the wall. 'It's near on half an hour late!'

'Surely it doesn't usually stop outside your office,' Jonah said, walking to the door with the marshal following.

A crowd was beginning to gather as they stepped out onto the sidewalk. The driver and guard climbed down from opposite sides of the box seat.

'There was a hold-up,' the driver yelled, in answer to questions as he looked for the marshal. 'No one hurt,' he added.

The door of the dusty stagecoach opened, and a young man climbed out. He was followed by a heavy-set man in a smart suit, and a travelling sales-man, then a tall, gangly man, who reached up to help a young woman down the steps. She wore a good-quality dress, now rather crumpled, and kept her face averted from the watchers.

'Why, that's Miss Louise!' Jonah exclaimed. He shoved his way through the gawping crowd, ducked under the hitching rail and jumped down into the street. 'Are you all right?' he asked anxiously, taking hold of her shoulders.

She flinched at first, then recognized him and relaxed a little. Green eyes filled with unshed tears.

'Did they hurt you?' Jonah asked softly, slipping one arm around her waist.

Miss Louise swallowed, then whispered, 'Take me home, please.'

CHAPTER TWO

Home for Miss Louise was a large, well-built house a little way up the other side of Panhandle Street. Jonah ignored the wide front door, with its well-polished brass knocker, and took Miss Louise to the kitchen door at the back. There they were met by the cook, Ken, who was chopping vegetables.

'Fetch Miss Jenny,' Jonah said. 'Then make some good, strong coffee.'

'Sure.' Ken wiped his hands on a towel, then hurried out.

Jonah led Louise from the kitchen, along a short, windowless corridor, and into a pleasant parlour that overlooked the yard and stables at the back of the house. There he sat her in a chintz-covered armchair, and sat himself at the plain dining table. Louise pulled a handkerchief from the pocket of her skirt and blew her nose vigorously as a few tears rolled down her face. Jonah handed her his own fine linen handkerchief and she mopped her face with it. His heart went out to her as she sat huddled and red-eyed in her spoiled finery.

'Whatever's happened, I'll do my best to help,' he promised the shivering woman.

The door opened, and Miss Jenny entered. Jonah stood up politely, and greeted her eye to eye, for she was remarkably tall, with glossy, dark hair braided into a neat coil on top of her head, adding to her height. She flashed a smile at Jonah, her brown eyes warm, then turned to Louise, crouching beside her chair.

'What happened?' she asked. 'I heard the stage was attacked.'

Louise swallowed, and nodded.

'And what happened to you?' Miss Jenny's voice was soft, but her face hardened as she put a gentle hand on the girl's shoulder.

Louise lifted her head, looking straight forward into space. 'One of the robbers . . . took me.' Her face contorted. 'He recognized me. He said it wouldn't matter none, as I was just a whore and I'd open up for anyone as had the money.'

'Didn't the men on the coach stand up for you?' Jonah demanded indignantly.

'The tall newspaperman, Robinson, he said something, an' he was nice to me afterwards, but the bandits had guns on them,' Louise told him.

20

Jonah frowned, his mouth drawing into a narrow line. 'Can't blame them for not wanting to tackle armed men, I guess,' he admitted. 'But that bandit had no right to take you against your will.'

Louise flushed. 'He wasn't really so bad. It hurts some but at least he didn't hit me.' Her voice grew increasingly bitter. 'It was the way the other people looked at me afterwards. They mostly acted like I wasn't there, or nothing had happened to me. That Mrs. Thompson got more sympathy than I did, and the bandits never even laid a finger on her.'

Jenny sighed. 'I'm sorry. You know that's the way lots of folk look at us. You can have tonight off and rest.'

Louise shook her head. 'I'll have a bath; that'll fix me up.'

'Jenny's right. You should take care of yourself,' Jonah said.

Louise looked him right in the eye. 'My ma and pa and brother died of the fever when I was eleven. Some neighbours took me in, but they made it clear I had to earn my keep. I scrubbed, cooked, cleaned and looked after the hens just to have old clothes and dry, stale food. When I got to fourteen, their son started on at me to sleep with him. When I refused, he said he'd tell folks I'd stolen goods and I'd be sent to jail. I figured that if I had to sleep with a man, I could get a better pay than hand-me-down clothes and leftover food.'

'I stole some money from them and bought a ticket to Kansas City. I went to the fanciest whore-house I could find and asked to work there. I've been taking care of myself ever since. So long as men pay me good money for sex, I'll sleep with them, but I'm saving it, so one day I can stop doing it, and won't need to rely on anyone to help me because I'll have enough money to keep me for the rest of my life.'

Jonah nodded. 'You've sure got grit; I reckon you'll make it. What do you mean to do with your-self when you quit this life?'

Louise paused, then smiled. 'Lie on satin sheets and eat cream-cakes,' she said firmly.

Jonah and Jenny laughed.

'That's as good an ambition as any, and better than most,' Jonah said.

Louise drew in a deep breath and let it out in a long sigh. 'Well, it won't happen unless I pick myself up and get on with it.' She rose and turned to Jenny. 'I really would like to have a bath, though.'

'I'll send Susie up with hot water when it's ready.'

'I'd better sponge and press these clothes,' Louise added, looking down at her outfit. She made an impatient sound. 'I forgot; they stole my brooch. It was a present from a nice gentleman in

Kansas City.' She stopped and sniffed suddenly, blinking back tears, then blew her nose fiercely. 'Thank you,' she said to Jonah, gesturing with the soggy handkerchief. 'I'll return this when it's clean.'

'There's no rush,' Jonah reassured her. 'I'm going to search for those sons-of-bitches who thought they could do what they liked to you. They'll learn different when I catch up with them.'

'I don't think you can shame him in the same way,' Louise said strongly. 'But iffen you hold him down, I'll hurt him. That will do.' With a nod to them both, she stalked from the room.

'Robinson?'

The tall newspaperman turned at the sound of his name. A handsome, well-dressed man rose from the green plush couch in the foyer of the Colorado Hotel, where Robinson was returning after settling his things in his room, and moved towards him. Robinson noted the matched guns with a quick glance and his reporter's instincts twitched in anticipation. He smiled as he shook the hand offered.

'I'm Jonah Durrell,' the handsome man said. 'I wanted to thank you for your kindness to Miss Louise, on the stage this afternoon.'

'You mean Miss Waterford, yeah?' Robinson replied. 'It was most unfortunate that that robber recognized her. Well, I don't know for sure if he was correct about her profession?'

'He was,' Jonah admitted. 'And it will be most unfortunate for him when I find him.' He gestured towards the hotel bar. 'Care for a drink?'

'Thank you.'

As Jonah went to the bar, Robinson chose a table in a quiet corner and sat down. Pulling notebook and pencil from his pocket, he made a few notes, then put them on the table. Jonah soon appeared with two beers, and put them down before sliding himself gracefully into the other chair. Robinson realized that he was sprawled inelegantly in his own, and made an effort to sit upright and pull in his long limbs. As he noted the other man adjusting the set of his gunbelt, Robinson suddenly remembered how he knew his name.

'Jonah Durrell, you're a manhunter, yeah?' Robinson asked. 'I saw your name in a report in a newspaper when I was passing through Denver last year.'

Jonah smiled. 'A Denver paper? I didn't know I was being spoken of that far from here. I mostly work in the San Juans.'

'I'm a correspondent for the *New-York Tribune*,' Robinson told him, his mind working fast. 'I should be most interested in hearing about your experiences, Mr. Durrell. I could make a most fascinating letter for the paper, yeah?'

'Would it include my picture?' Jonah asked, a little eagerly.

'I could certainly send a photograph for the artists to see, but it would be the editor's decision.'

'I'm sure he'd agree. After all, a picture of me is bound to increase circulation amongst your female readers,' Jonah said, with a shameless smile.

Robinson was taken aback for a moment, then saw the humour in Jonah's dark eyes. He laughed. 'If they don't want your picture for my letter, they could use it to advertise hair tonic, yeah?'

Jonah laughed too. 'If they want to use it for an advertisement, I'd better get paid for it.'

With the ice broken, they both sampled their beer. Jonah put his glass back on the table.

'I'm happy to talk to you, Robinson, for your paper, but I'd like some information from you in return. I want to find the men who held up the stage – particularly the one who raped Miss Louise. I need all the information you can give me about the hold-up and the bandits.'

Robinson nodded, and exchanged his glass for his notebook. 'I wrote down my impressions immediately afterwards. The men wore bandannas over their faces, so I couldn't make out much of their features, but I recorded what I could see, to tell the law, afterwards.'

'Good.' Jonah produced a small notebook of his

own and a silver pencil. 'May I copy your notes?'

'Only if you read shorthand, I'm afraid.' Robinson flipped open his notebook.

Jonah studied the series of squiggles. 'My father writes like that.'

'Is he a reporter?'

'No. A doctor.'

By the time Robinson's detailed notes had been transcribed into Jonah's neat longhand, the beers were almost finished. Jonah read the notes back to himself and thought for a few moments before speaking.

'The bandits had two mules with pack saddles with them?'

Robinson nodded. 'They went for that money-chest right away, yeah? They didn't look in the rear boot or at the goods stowed on top. They didn't even take that much from the passengers, just the cash money we had on us, and Gibson's gold watch. They didn't bother with my old silver one,' he added, indicating the silver chain that showed a watch in his waistcoat pocket. 'Fortunately, I had the wit to hide the substance of my cash money inside the coach and they didn't bother searching that. However, I believe that they were acquainted with the fact of the money-chest being on the stagecoach.'

'I was thinking that myself,' Jonah agreed. 'So how did they know it was there?'

'It would be useful to know who owned the chest. I expect it must be a bank or a mine to need that much gold coin,' Robinson said. 'If we knew where it was destined for, we could find out who knew it was going to be on that stage. Unless of course it was a regular delivery, for a payday, yeah?'

'You'd have to be as dumb as a shovel to put your payroll on the same coach every month,' Jonah remarked. 'Then again, some folks are, even them that run a business. I reckon Marshal Tapton will know where the money was set for by now; I can ask him.' He paused and considered for a moment. 'Folk might talk to a newspaperman that wouldn't talk to a manhunter. If you're willing to help me out some here, you could get some fine material for your papers.'

Robinson's smile was wide and engaging. 'I'd sure admire to work with you, Mr. Durrell.'

'It's Jonah to my friends.'

'My first name's Hulton, but my friends call me Robinson.' The newspaperman held his hand out, and Jonah shook it.

'Let's go see the marshal, then,' Jonah said. He finished up his beer, Robinson following his good example, and they left the hotel together.

Marshal Tapton told them that the stolen money was the payroll of the Red Horse Mine. He also gave them a list of the items stolen from the passengers: Miss Louise's brooch wasn't included, as she hadn't spoken to the marshal on arriving in town. Neither Jonah nor Robinson recalled its loss, remembering only that she'd been raped. Robinson spent a while looking through the marshal's wanted notices, but he didn't confidently recognize any of the men described.

As they strolled back to the Hotel Colorado, where Jonah was also staying, the afternoon sunlight was turning to evening. The soft glow of oil lamps was showing in windows along Panhandle Street. A few stores had closed, but others were still open to get trade from those who had been busy during the daylight hours. Music and voices carried from the saloons along the street, competing with the ever-present rumble of ore-processing machinery in the nearest mines. Jonah indicated a tall, well-built house on the other side of the street.

'That's Miss Jenny's parlour house,' he said.

As they looked, a young woman dressed in a modest, maid's outfit appeared at one of the ground floor windows to draw the deep, crimson curtains. She carefully left a small gap to show a red-shaded lamp within.

'It looks a regular, respectable establishment,' Robinson commented.

'Miss Jenny runs a very respectable house of ill-repute,' Jonah answered. 'And she's one of the finest women I know. She does like her visitors to have an introduction or recommendation, but I'm happy to speak for you.'

'Oh, er . . . when were you planning to visit?'

'Tonight.' Jonah glanced at his companion. 'I beg your pardon if you object to visiting parlour houses?'

Robinson shook his head. 'Well, no. I do feel the need of a little – sport – now and again and I find it less awkward to attend a place where it's a straightforward business transaction, rather than trying to attract the company of a saloon girl, or suchlike.'

'Miss Jenny runs a clean place, looks after her girls and helps them get a bit of education if they need it, so they can marry well or set up a business of their own.'

'It appears that you are well acquainted with Miss Jenny?' Robinson enquired.

Jonah nodded. 'From when I first came to Motherlode this spring. A saloonkeeper was trying to scare her into letting him into her business, but I helped her out. Only helped her, mind; she's sure got grit. She's someone any man would admire to know, and a friend worth having. I like to visit her place just for the company.'

'That business with the saloonkeeper sounds like a story worth hearing,' Robinson prompted.

Jonah laughed. 'Forget about your newspaper articles for a piece. Let's get a bite to eat, get ourselves bathed and gussied up, and go enjoy some

29

pleasant company.'

So saying, he led the way into the hotel, Robinson following with a last glance over his shoulder at the house with the red lamp in the window.

CHAPTER THREE

It was fully dark by the time the two men crossed the street again. Motherlode was in its full night-time swing, with the saloons, dance hall and pool hall all doing good business. Robinson paid little attention to the general hubbub as Jonah rapped the polished, brass door knocker. A smartly-dressed black man opened the door and greeted Jonah by name in friendly terms.

'Good evening, Albert,' Jonah replied as they entered. 'This is a friend of mine.'

Albert nodded at Robinson and indicated a door to the right of the hall. 'Please come through, gentlemen.'

The parlour house was as well appointed as the hotel, and cosier. The hall had striped wallpaper, decorated with tasteful silhouettes of female heads. A small, mahogany table held a vase of wild flowers and an ashtray, and the air carried the mingled scents of perfume, tobacco and furniture polish. Someone was playing a waltz on a piano in a room partially visible through an archway on the left of the hall.

They followed Albert through to a room where half a dozen or so young women were gathered. The carpet, draperies, wallpaper and ornaments all combined for a comforting, homelike feel, aided by the light sound of the women's voices. Even the fact that the pictures were of naked women didn't stop Robinson from suddenly being aware of the lack of pleasant company, especially female company, in his everyday life. One of the women rose as they entered, and he turned towards her, then simply stared for a few seconds in surprise. Fortunately, she was approaching Jonah first, and Robinson had time to collect himself before she turned to him, her eyes almost on a level with his own.

'Miss Jenny, this is my friend, Hulton F. Robinson,' Jonah made the introduction. 'He's agreed to help me in finding the men who attacked Miss Louise.'

Robinson took Miss Jenny's hand and bowed. 'Pleased to meet you.'

He had never before met a woman so close to his own height and it felt downright odd to him. Jenny, however, seemed quite comfortable with her height. As Robinson politely tried to conceal his reaction, he noticed a mischievous gleam in her dark eyes that suggested she was amused by his discomfort, rather than embarrassed.

'I'm delighted to meet someone I can talk to without both of us getting a crick in our necks, yeah?' Robinson added, with a smile.

Jenny laughed, acknowledging the joke. 'It does make a change,' she agreed.

'How is Miss Waterford?' Robinson asked, more seriously.

'She's fine, thankfully,' Jenny answered. 'In fact, she's in the dining room right now, with a gentleman. I suggested she rest tonight, but she wouldn't. She's got a lot of grit. Louise told me of your kindness, and I want to thank you for that.'

'I wish I could have done more – stopped it from happening in the first place.'

'From what I understand, you didn't have any choice. It would have been plumb foolish of you to take on armed road agents,' Jenny said.

'I guess it was just bad luck that that bandit recognized her,' Robinson said.

Jenny nodded. 'I'm just glad she wasn't hurt worse. But you, at least, treated her like a real person afterwards, and didn't just pretend that nothing had happened, or that she didn't deserve sympathy. As a thank you, everything tonight is on the house, as our guest.'

'That's very kind of you.' Robinson wondered

guiltily if he'd have treated Miss Louise differently if he'd known for certain earlier that she was a prostitute.

Jonah had been looking across the hall into the music parlour; now he politely interrupted the conversation.

'Excuse me, I see you have a professor at the piano. I can hear Miss Sandy in there and I'd like to see if she's free for a dance?'

'I believe she is,' Jenny answered, smiling. She put her hand on Jonah's shoulder. 'I'm sure she'll be pleased to see you.'

With a warm smile and a polite nod, Jonah went through to the other room.

'Now then, Mr. Robinson,' Jenny continued. 'Would you like to mix generally, or shall I introduce you to one of my boarders?'

'Um. . . .' Robinson looked around at the women.

There was an olive-skinned girl, with a lovely smile and corkscrews of dark hair trailing loosely from a bun. Beside her was a slender girl with pale skin and flaxen hair which was crowned with a spray of tiny flowers, but otherwise fell in loose waves to below her waist. Opposite was a beautiful woman with dark hair in a coiled braid on the back of her head.

'I'll defer to your judgement, Miss Jenny.'

She smiled reassuringly and led him across the

room. 'Mr. Robinson, I'd like you to meet Miss Erica.'

Miss Erica held out her hand. 'Please, sit beside me so we can talk.' With her other hand, she patted the empty space beside herself on the two-seater sofa. Miss Erica was a dark-haired beauty with a clear, creamy complexion and blue eyes that shone with the love of life.

'Your accent?' Robinson said, as he sat.

She laughed lightly. 'Yes, I'm English.'

She sounded different to the other English people Robinson had met, and he guessed accurately that it was an upper-class accent. 'I'm sorry,' he apologized. 'You must hear that all the time, yeah?'

'I hear all kinds of accents here and they all sound as foreign to me as I do to you,' she replied. 'You sound rather like Jonah. Are you from Vermont, too?'

'Rhode Island, so both are part of New England,' he said with some pride.

'I never saw New England,' Erica told him. 'I landed in New York and came west. Is it beautiful country?'

'Why, yes.' Robinson considered for a few moments. 'It isn't grand, like the scenery here in Colorado, yeah, or endless like the prairies. It's smaller in scale, but I reckon it's pretty swell.'

'Describe it for me, please,' Erica asked, her

lovely face turned to him with flattering, and genuine attention.

Robinson began to describe his home town, drawn on by Erica's questions. He began to relax, helped by good wine, good conversation and the social atmosphere of the parlour. His previous visits to prostitutes had been more a matter of physical need and the women had been a pleasant means of satisfying that need. Robinson had never learned anything about them as people in their own right. Talking with Miss Erica was a comfortable, fascinating experience as she talked about her impression of America as an immigrant and the cultural differences.

Things got livelier when they joined Jonah and the vivacious Miss Sandy in the well-appointed dining room for an excellent meal. Miss Sandy proved to have an earthy sense of humour and lowered the tone of the conversation with great style. It was one of the most entertaining evenings Robinson had ever had, and after they finished eating, it seemed the most natural thing in the world to accompany Erica up the stairs to her bedroom, where the pleasure became more personal.

Robinson and Jonah met again the next morning at breakfast in their hotel's dining room. Robinson felt a little awkward at first, in the clean light of a new morning. However, other than a vague enquiry about whether the newspaperman

had had a good night, Jonah showed no inclina-
tion to discuss anything that had happened in the
brothel's bedrooms. Robinson realized he had
somewhat misjudged his new friend. Some other
men he'd met had been happy to discuss the abil-
ities and attributes of prostitutes, sometimes
almost as if comparing horses hired from a livery
stable. He guessed that Jonah wasn't reticent
through embarrassment or lack of self-confidence;
he simply respected the women and himself.

Instead, the conversation was about plans for
the day, in relation to the attack on the stagecoach,
and Miss Louise. Jonah decided to visit the Red
Horse Mine where the stolen payroll had been destined, as he'd been there before. Robinson offered
to go to the stagecoach company and talk to the
owner.

'I'd like to know if his drivers have seen those
bandits before, yeah, or if payrolls have been
stolen from them before?' Robinson said.

'The marshal didn't mention any other stagecoach robberies,' Jonah said. 'Though it may be
that he just didn't think to,' he added. 'The
Golden West Company's not been in Motherlode
long; it wasn't here when I first came in the
spring.' He thought for a moment. 'I reckon it
must have been set up in July.'

'Two months. They've done well to get a contract to deliver payrolls that soon,' Robinson said.

'Unless there was another company that quit, yeah?'

'There wasn't a stage line in Motherlode before,' Jonah told him. 'There's one runs between Durango, Silverton, Ouray and Montrose, but it's harder to run east-west.'

'The Golden West runs between Telluride and Animas Forks,' Robinson said.

'Plenty of mines along that route,' Jonah mused. 'If they could get regular contracts to deliver payrolls and some goods, then that would help.'

'I'll find out what I can,' Robinson promised. 'Folks that have done well like to talk about their success,' he added shrewdly. 'And if the listener is a newspaperman, they can become quite loquacious.'

Jonah smiled. 'You go get the owner of the Golden West to loquate as well as you can, and I'll go call on the Red Horse Mine and get the other end of the story.'

Some fifteen minutes later, Robinson was at the offices of the Golden West Stagecoach Company. Stable blocks and barns enclosed most of the company's yard, with the modest office tucked in a corner by the high fence that separated the yard from the street. There was hammering from a workshop, and a sudden hiss, accompanied by the smell of singeing, as a hot shoe was applied to a horse's hoof at the forge. Robinson paused to watch a large, heavyset man stacking bales of straw. The man lifted the bales as though they weighed nothing, making a tidy stack under a sloping roof adjacent to the stables. He paused briefly to stare at Robinson from an inscrutable, Slavic face, then returned to his labours.

Mildly unsettled by the look, Robinson knocked on the office door, and entered.

A quick glance showed him a well-appointed office, with a good-sized filing cabinet, a heavy safe and a substantial, leather-topped desk. The man behind the desk had an equally prosperous look to match his surroundings. He was stocky and powerful in build, almost to the point of being overweight. His face and balding scalp were pink and shining, with the hair at the sides of his head shaved so short as to be almost invisible. Blue eyes and a smile as he greeted Robinson, made him look like a genial gnome from a fairy story.

'Mr. Millard?' Robinson asked.

'Certainly, sir. How may I help you?' the businessmen answered, indicating a seat on Robinson's side of the desk.

'I'm Hulton F. Robinson, correspondent for the *New-York Tribune*. I was travelling on the stage that was robbed yesterday, yeah?' Robinson sat down.

Millard's smile abruptly faded. 'Terms of the company state that passengers travel at their own risk.' He suddenly looked decidedly thuggish.

'Oh, I understand that. I'm not here to make a complaint,' Robinson explained hastily. 'I travel a lot on the stages, but until now, I've taken them rather for granted. Yesterday's unfortunate experience made me think about the risks in setting up and running a stagecoach company. I feel it would make a fascinating subject for a letter, or a series of letters, to the *Tribune*. I was hoping that you could help me, yeah? You must have a great understanding of the subject.'

'I have been somewhat successful,' Millard admitted modestly. As he shifted in his chair, sunlight flashed off the stickpin in his tie, and caught Robinson's eye. Millard saw him blink and gave a little laugh. 'I do apologize; I had no intention of dazzling you.' He moved his hand to briefly cover the diamond-tipped stickpin, giving Robinson a glimpse of the diamond-set cufflink he wore.

'It's very beautiful,' Robinson said, trying to imagine how much the tiepin and cufflink set would cost. It occurred to him that Jonah would probably know.

Millard smiled. 'I'm afraid that jewels are my weakness; I even named my daughters after them.'

Robinson had got out his notebook and pencil without even thinking about it. 'Really, which jewels?'

'The eldest is Opal, she's eighteen. Her sisters

40

are Pearl, Ruby and Amethyst. I think of Amethyst as the baby, but she's nine now, not really a baby anymore.'

'Those are pretty names,' Robinson said politely. He realized that he was making notes and looked over at Millard. 'A newspaperman's habit, yeah?' he said, gesturing with the notebook and pointing at it with the pencil. 'I can leave the names of your family out if you wish, but readers like the personal detail. I believe that readers will be charmed by your daughters' names, yeah?'

'I guess a whole family of jewels must be rather uncommon?' Millard asked, with a nice degree of modestly-concealed pride. 'If I'd had more daughters, I was considering Emerald, Amber and Topaz as names,' he added thoughtfully.

Robinson wondered briefly what Millard would have named a son. Jet, perhaps? Or Jasper? He pulled his thoughts back to the matter at hand.

'You look to have a mighty fine yard out there,' he said. 'Everything a coach line might require, including your own forge.'

Millard warmed to the praise. 'Indeed, we do. "No foot, no horse" is perfectly true, so I prefer to have our own smith to tend to the horses. With my own man, I can be sure of getting a skilled job, plus, he's available whenever necessary, so we don't have to wait at a public forge if a horse has cast a shoe. The smith also makes fittings for the coaches and helps the carpenters keep them in good repair.'

As Millard continued to talk about his company with quiet self-satisfaction, Robinson brought the conversation round to the early days of his business. Although Millard had only been operating from Motherlode for three months, he'd run stagecoach companies in four other towns over the years, starting in Missouri before moving west after the war, and then around Colorado.

'Have you encountered much trouble with road agents before?' Robinson asked.

'Now and again,' Millard said. 'The attack that you, unfortunately, endured, was the first one since moving to Motherlode.'

'Are your drivers here the same ones you employed back in Cañon City?'

Millard shook his head. 'No, I wanted drivers who knew the local trails.'

'They didn't recognize the bandits at all, did they? If the bandits operate locally too, they might have robbed those drivers before, yeah?'

'No, I'm afraid my men were unable to give any useful information to the marshal.'

Robinson made a note of that. 'Do you carry valuable loads like payrolls to a regular schedule – the same day each month?' he asked.

'No. Each mine needs its payroll at roughly the same time each month,' Millard replied. 'But we arrange with them for it to be transported on different days, and at different times.'

'How do you make those arrangements with the mines?'

'When we get a new contract, I visit the mines and we work out a schedule for the next six months at a time. Each mine contacts its bank when it wants its payroll put on the stage and copies of the schedule are kept locked away securely.' Millard gestured at the stout, iron safe fixed to the wall of his office.

'How far in advance do employees learn that they will be taking a payroll?'

Millard frowned thoughtfully, his face turning thuggish. 'I don't tell them, they find out when the guards from the bank bring it to them. And I think we're done discussing details of our security arrangements.'

Robinson nodded, not wanting to provoke Millard. 'I'm sure grateful to you for your time. I've got a lot of interesting material here.' He smiled. 'And I swear there won't be anything about how you arrange security in the article. I was just asking for my own curiosity, after witnessing the attack, yeah?'

'I'm sure you'll write a terrific piece for your paper,' Millard said generously. 'Would it be long before it appears?' He tried to be casual about his question.

'A few weeks at least and I can't guarantee it will be printed,' Robinson said, putting away notebook and pencil. 'But I believe it will. I may need to ask some more questions, once I start writing,' he added. He fully intended to write a letter about the stagecoach business, but it was good to have an excuse to come back if he and Jonah had more questions about the robbery and the attack on Miss Louise.

'You can be sure of my help,' Millard assured him.

They shook hands and Robinson left, heading back to his hotel. He wanted to start getting down ideas for letters about Jonah as well as the stage-coach company. A sudden thought caused him to stop in his tracks, making other people swerve round him on the busy sidewalk of Panhandle Street. Oblivious to the curses directed at him, Robinson took out his notebook and glanced at the notes he'd just made. His memory was right. Millard's first stagecoach line had run for seven years in Missouri. He'd then operated from Denver for three years, before moving to Boulder for another three, and Cañon City for just two years, before relocating here to Motherlode. Why should someone with a successful business just up sticks and move to another place, with the expense of setting up new premises and the trouble of finding new contracts and suppliers? Millard

44

didn't seem to have failed in the other cities: he had money. Robinson shrugged; maybe Millard just liked new challenges. Striding out again, he made his way back to the hotel.

CHAPTER FOUR

There was a flash of red as a male crossbill swooped across the trail just ahead. Jonah's horse pricked its ears and jumped sideways in pretend fright.

'Steady, Cirrus,' Jonah chuckled, as his legs and hands automatically steadied the dapple-grey and sent it on again at a steady trot.

The horse had been doing no more than letting off a little steam on this fine, fall morning. Jonah was in pretty good spirits himself. He'd quit his medical studies for adventure out west and after a year of punching cattle, had ended up here in Colorado. Jonah had fallen in love with the green fields and trees, the grey and red mountains, topped with sparkling snow all year round, and the fresh, clear air that made the most distant peaks as sharp as the nearest. The towns and mills that were springing up made ugly blots on the landscape, staining the sky with their smoke, but Jonah enjoyed the pleasures of town life as well. His current line of work enabled him to enjoy both the towns and the country, and to earn good money, too. Although he didn't realize it himself, part of Jonah's charm came from his own contentment with life.

Jonah reached the Red Horse Mine before midday. He watered Cirrus and made his horse comfortable before approaching the office buildings. The clerk remembered him from a visit earlier in the year, and after a short wait, Jonah was shown into the manager's office. He greeted the manager, Mr. Rooney, and sat down in front of the dark-wood, polished desk.

'Jonah Durrell,' Rooney mused, studying Jonah with shrewd, pale eyes. 'I've heard your name a few times. You're a bounty hunter.'

Jonah nodded and smiled. 'I am. Forgive me for intruding on your time. I know you must be busy.' He indicated the sheets of paper stacked in tidy piles on the desk. 'I want to find the men who attacked the stage and stole your payroll yesterday.'

'The management of the Red Horse Mine haven't yet decided whether to offer a reward for catching the criminals, or for the return of the money,' Rooney said. 'And we're not in the business of hiring anyone ourselves to find either.'

'I'm not doing it just for money,' Jonah said. 'No

doubt the state will put a reward on the men, if they haven't got one already, and I shouldn't mind iffen the mine owners felt all generous to someone who helped them,' he added honestly. 'But a couple of friends of mine were on that stage, and I want to bring in the outlaw scum for them, especially for Miss Louise.'

'I heard they raped a whore who was travelling on the stage.'

'They raped a *woman* who was travelling on that stage. That's all Miss Louise was doing, travelling; they sure as sin didn't have the right to take her against her will, regardless of how she has to earn money to live.'

Rooney opened his mouth to say something, but after a look at Jonah's face, hesitated before saying anything. 'Well, I . . . guess that that's none of my business. If you're not asking for payment for hunting the outlaws, what do you want here?'

Jonah took a deep breath, letting his anger seep away 'According to one of the passengers on the stage, the outlaws went straight for your payroll. They took a few things from the passengers, but they didn't bother searching the rest of the luggage for anything valuable. All they were really interested in was the payroll. It seems to me like they knew it was on that stagecoach.'

Rooney frowned. 'You think someone from the stage company tipped them off?'

'I don't know,' Jonah admitted. 'I'm going to look into that.' He didn't feel the time was right to admit to a newspaperman being involved in the case. 'But there's a chance it could have been someone from this company.'

'I keep the schedule of payroll deliveries in my safe,' Rooney said. He leaned back and drummed his fingers on the desk. 'No one could get it out of the safe without I knew about it, but it's possible someone could have seen it when it was out.'

'One of your clerks?' Jonah suggested.

Rooney snorted. 'Not one of the clerks, they ain't got the gumption. Wouldn't be clerks if they did.'

Jonah chose not to comment on that. He thought for a moment. 'If someone did tip the robbers off, they did it for a reason. Most likely for a share of the money but it could have been someone with a grudge against the mine, or you personally. Has there been any bad blood between you and someone recently? Or anyone gotten themselves fired?'

Rooney stared piercingly at Jonah, as if wondering whether to take offence. After a few moments, he relaxed. 'Bert Wood,' he said abruptly. 'A waggoner. I told him to skin out of here last week. I warned him about not looking after his horses properly, but he didn't listen.'

'Any idea where he might have gone?'

'Don't know and don't rightly care.'

Jonah nodded. 'I'll speak to some of the other wagoners, if I may. Might get some idea about where he'd go, from them.'

'Just don't get in their way.' Rooney hauled out his pocket watch and glanced at the face. 'I got to get on,' he said abruptly.

Jonah stood gracefully. 'Thank you for your time, Mr. Rooney.' He nodded to the manager, who was already reaching for a folder, and left. Jonah spoke to a couple of the Red Horse Mine wagoners, and quickly found out that Bert Wood had not been a popular person. The first man flatly stated that he didn't know where Wood had gone, and didn't damn well care. The second one gave a rough description of Wood and summed him up briefly.

'You'll smell him afore you see him. Neglects hisself like he done his horses. He'd rather drink and gamble than do an ounce of work, and I swear to God, he'd piss on a fire to put it out, rather'n fetch water.'

Jonah wrinkled his nose at the imagined smell, thanked his informant, and went to fetch his own, well cared-for horse.

The simplest thing was to look in the saloons and gambling dens of the nearest town, so Jonah headed to Animas Forks. It was a small place, dominated by the two mills on the nearby slopes. Two stores, three saloons, a laundry, a stable, a post office and a hotel made up the centre of the town, surrounded by upwards of thirty rough, lumber shacks and a half dozen more that were still half canvas. The mills rumbled as they processed ore, and mules brayed in counterpoint to the banging of hammers as building work went on. The town smelt of manure, smoke and fresh-cut pine. They were the sounds and smells of the frontier being developed, and new lives being made out in the new territories. It was all so raw and vibrant in contrast to the neat and calm ways back east where Jonah had grown up. As the newspapers said, this was the land of opportunity, and Jonah felt himself to be part of it.

Halting outside the first saloon he reached, Jonah dismounted and hitched his horse to the rail in front. There were no sidewalks here, but the earth at the sides of the street was packed hard after the summer. Jonah entered the saloon slowly, giving his eyes time to adjust to the dim light as he looked around. This was the newest saloon of the three, and the simplest. Although it was noon, lamps were lit at the far end of the narrow room. When the golden pine of the walls darkened with age and smoke, it would be a gloomy place to spend the evening. Jonah strolled to the bar and asked for a quality brand of whiskey. As he'd expected, the saloon didn't stock it. He shook his head at the offer of some dubious, brown spirit that claimed to be whiskey, and strolled out again, taking the time to unobtrusively study the few patrons. None of them looked or smelt like Bert Wood.

Two doors along was the fanciest saloon of the three in town. Jonah decided to leave it until last. Wood probably preferred someplace where the liquor and women were cheaper, and it didn't sound as though he'd be too fussy about the overall standards of either. The saloon a little way down on the other side of the street had dust-freckled windows and the paint on its frontage was already weathered and faded.

Heading inside, Jonah strolled to the bar, taking his time as there was no bartender in sight. A few of the tables were occupied, and a burly man in a plaid shirt was playing a waltz on a piano in the corner. As Jonah hitched his elbow on the bar, a saloon girl in a yellow, satin dress approached him.

'Hello, handsome,' she drawled. Jonah turned to look at her, and as she saw him clearly, her eyes widened. 'Oh, my!' Her voice shot up by an octave or so.

Jonah smiled in good humour, making her flutter her hand to her generously exposed bosom. 'Can I help you?' he enquired politely.

'Oh ... I ... um.' She swallowed and took a deep breath.

It took a little effort for Jonah to keep a straight face; she looked like someone who had picked up a dollar in the street and found it was actually a hundred-dollar bill. Jonah let the saloon girl flounder for a minute, then smiled kindly. 'I'm not stopping long, so I'm not looking for company right now.' He dug a couple of dollars from his pocket and tucked them into the front of her cheap dress. With a gentle but firm hand on her shoulder, he turned her and propelled her away.

As there was still no one at the bar, Jonah strolled casually across the room towards the piano player. He carefully wandered close to a table where a man sat by himself, nurturing a beer bottle and trying to make a roll up stub last as long as possible. The other people in the bar smelt no worse than labourers usually did. This man not only reeked of stale sweat and smoke, Jonah picked up a tang of urine that made his nose wrinkle. His hair was lank and scurfy, his vast beard held fragments of food and cigarette ash and his clothes were stiff with dirt.

'Bert Wood?'

The burly man blinked and glowered at Jonah. 'Whaddya want?'

'Just a couple of questions. I'll get you . . .' Jonah's offer of beer was interrupted.

'I ain't talking,' Wood growled. 'I ain't done nothing.'

'I'll . . .' Jonah reached for his billfold to get a few dollars.

'No!' Wood erupted out of his chair, sending it flying, and lashed out with a punch.

Jonah had been expecting trouble, but not quite so soon. Even so, he easily stepped aside, deflecting the blow to his right. As Wood came level with him, Jonah spun and delivered a sharp jab to the ribs with his left hand, bringing a grunt from the big man.

Wood spun with surprising speed and lashed out with two quick punches. Jonah dodged one but caught the other on his shoulder. Wood gave a yell of triumph at his success, and closed in with a sharp jab to Jonah's face. Jonah knew how fast the big man could move now, and was ready. He dodged again, the solid fist barely missing his cheek, and threw his weight into smashing the heel of his hand into the wagoner's nose. He felt it break, and Wood cried out as he retreated, but the big man still flailed a blow that caught Jonah painfully on his upper arm.

They separated for a moment, blood tricking down Wood's face. Jonah caught his breath, holding his fists up defensively as he considered things. He'd underestimated how fast Wood could move. The wagoner was nearly as tall as Jonah, and much more powerful and heavy. Getting beaten up by him would be a painful experience, and leave Jonah vulnerable to anyone else who fancied proving himself against a manhunter. As he thought, Jonah moved, taking the opportunity for a quick glance at his surroundings. He met Wood's gaze again, and smiled confidently.

'I guess I've broken your nose,' he remarked. 'Still, no need to worry. You ain't got any good looks to lose anyhow.'

Wood cursed, and yelled, 'I'm gonna knock you sky west and crooked!' As others watching yelled encouragement, he rushed towards Jonah.

As Jonah had intended, Wood aimed for his face. Jonah sidestepped slightly, ducked the blows and drove a punch into Wood's belly. As the big man grunted explosively, Jonah spun around him and punched him in the kidneys. Wood yelled and lashed out backwards as he turned. A brawny arm caught Jonah as he was moving and slightly off-balance. He staggered backwards and fell, but kept rolling. Wood yelled again as the watchers cheered encouragement, and closed in. Jonah got his feet under himself and started to rise.

He didn't straighten fully though. Wood's fist went over his head as Jonah lunged forward, head-butting Wood hard in the stomach. Wood gasped out beery breath and staggered away, flailing at his opponent. He hit Jonah hard enough to stagger him slightly as they separated. Jonah got clear and straightened fully as he turned. He took a few moments to recover himself as Wood also caught his balance. The wagoner was red in the face and had no breath to spare for insults, but the aggression in his eyes had changed to fury.

Jonah danced lightly from foot to foot for a moment, then came in fast, his eyes on Wood's face. The big man braced in place to meet him, fists up, ready to meet Jonah's. A fraction before he got within reach, Jonah stopped dead and swung his right foot up in a precise kick. The toe of his boot caught Wood right in the testicles. Wood flushed darker red, then went white, dropping his guard to clutch at his groin as he made a high, wailing sound. Jonah acted quickly, landing a heavy punch on Wood's ear, then mashing his nose again with his other fist. Wood staggered back and collapsed, whimpering and gasping.

Jonah took a few moments to get his breath back, smooth his hair and straighten his clothing. Seeing that the fight was over, the other patrons lost interest and sat down again. Jonah stood over the groaning wagoner.

'Now, let's start again. How about you answer some questions and iffen I reckon I got enough truth, I'll fix up that broken nose for you?'

Taking a moan as an answer, Jonah started to question Wood about what he'd been doing since leaving the Red Horse Mine.

CHAPTER FIVE

There was a fragrant smell of cooking when Millard arrived home that evening. As he closed the front door behind himself, his wife, Mary glided from the parlour. She was wearing a stylish, glossy dress of deep green, and he noticed she'd chosen the gold necklace, earrings and bracelet with little diamond and emerald flowers to enhance her clothes. The yellow lamplight disguised the traces of grey among her carefully-styled dark-blonde hair, and to Millard, she still looked far too young and trim to be the mother of four daughters, the oldest now eighteen.

'Hello, my dear.' Millard's usual greeting was warm.

Mary presented her cheek to be kissed. 'You're a little late,' she said. 'Susan is almost ready to serve dinner.'

'I was interrupted this morning,' Millard excused himself as he took his coat off and handed it to his wife. 'There's a newspaperman in town, who writes for the *New-York Tribune*. He came to interview me about running a stagecoach company.'

'Really? Would anyone be interested in that?' Mary hung up the coat as Millard eased off his boots.

Millard frowned slightly. 'Robinson seemed to think so. He said I was a good example of what grit and enterprise can achieve, and talked about how valuable the stage lines are. It will be terrific publicity, Mary,' he added.

'Well, it won't cost anything, and I guess it can't hurt,' Mary said, leading the way into the parlour.

The curtains were already drawn and the warm light from two oil lamps bathed the room, reflected back from a pair of large mirrors. The light sparkled from the jewelry worn by his four daughters. Opal and Pearl rose and walked with studied grace towards their father. Ruby looked up from the schoolbook she was studying, rolled her eyes, and put her nose in her book again. Amethyst leapt from her chair, scattering the house of cards she'd been building, and raced across the room, greeting her father with a squeal and a hug. Millard laughed and squeezed her in return.

'Amethyst, how many times must I tell you to be more ladylike?' Mary chastised her daughter. 'You're nearly ten now; you don't want to draw attention to yourself by behaving like a boy.'

Amethyst flushed, for she was shy and hated attention from anyone outside her family. She released her hold on her father and was swept aside by the arrival of the two oldest girls.

'Oh, Papa, there's going to be a dance!' Opal exclaimed breathlessly. 'A dance at last: it's just too, too exciting! I'll need a new dress, I simply can't wear that old green organdie again.'

'That's because you've got fatter again,' Pearl said tartly. 'You need to pull your corset tighter.'

Opal was statuesque and looked well in the fashionable bustle dresses: Pearl was willowy and wore an exaggerated bustle with layers of flounces to compensate. Ignoring her sister, Opal opened her green eyes wider as she beseeched her father. 'There's a lovely, green, silk muslin in the draper's store. It would make such an *utterly* charming dress and it would go so nicely with this lovely ring,' she added shrewdly, holding up her right hand to show off the ring with the green opal, set with emeralds either side.

'There's a deep-blue silk that would set off my pearl brooch so well, if I could have a dress made of it, please, Papa,' Pearl weighed in, smiling sweetly as she always did for her father, though rarely for her older sister.

Millard patted both girls fondly on the shoulder. 'Well, I had a little luck recently, so I think I could manage new dresses for my jewels.' As Opal and Pearl exclaimed their thanks, he glanced over at Ruby. She was concentrating on her book, her mouth moving slightly as she memorized information. Millard smiled indulgently: she was only thirteen and there was still time for her to develop an interest in clothes and womanly things.

'Oh, I hope there'll be some nice, young men to dance with,' Pearl said, clutching her hands together.

'There won't be anyone worth marrying.' Opal pouted. 'This is such a backwoods place, Papa. Can't we please, please move to somewhere like Denver? It's so hard to be in style, somewhere like this, and there's no one worthwhile to see you anyway.'

'You girls must be grateful for the things you already have,' Mary said. 'You've been promised new dresses for the dance and that's enough for now. Dinner is ready,' she added. 'For Heaven's sake, Ruby, put that book away before you ruin your eyes, and come and eat dinner.'

Millard smiled fondly as his daughters obediently filed out of the parlour after their mother. His family was a sight he never grew tired of.

Back at his hotel that evening, Jonah ordered a

hot bath in his room. He was naturally fastidious, but the warm water also soothed his muscles after the fight earlier. Afterwards, he shaved and dressed with his usual care, spending a few happy minutes choosing his clothes for the evening. Giving his hair a last brush, Jonah studied himself in the mirror. Not a trace of the fight showed on his face; the only flaw was the small scar on his right cheek, where he'd been hit by a piece of flying glass earlier in the year while defending Miss Jenny's place. Jonah didn't mind the scar in the slightest, regarding it as a small price to pay for helping the women. He turned his head from side to side, looking at himself from different angles, then laughed at himself and left the room.

Jonah found Robinson in the hotel bar. The newspaperman was sprawled untidily on an upholstered bench seat, his notepad and pencil on the table in front of him. When he saw Jonah, Robinson waved and sat up, gathering his long limbs together and giving the impression of a bundle of sticks being straightened up and neatened. Jonah brought two beers from the bar and sat down with a conscious grace.

'Did you learn anything interesting?' Robinson asked eagerly.

'I learned not to get into a fight with a feller that looks like a grizzly bear and smells like a month-dead buffalo,' Jonah replied. As Robinson's eyes widened, Jonah indicated the notepad and pencil on the table. The newspaperman snatched them up, and made notes as Jonah told his tale.

'He got himself hurt for no good reason,' Jonah concluded. 'When he finally talked, he'd just been bumming around town since leaving the mine, earning a few dollars collecting trash and digging outhouse holes, then wasting them on cheap liquor and card games.'

'So, the mine seems to be a dead-end then?'

Jonah nodded. 'Did you learn anything about Millard this morning?'

'Oh, yes.' Robinson flipped back through the pages of his notebook. He told Jonah about the security arrangements between the stagecoach company and the mines.

'Sounds pretty good,' Jonah mused. 'You're sure the bandits knew about the payroll in advance?'

Robinson nodded. 'They went straight for it.'

'Then unless it was a really lucky guess, someone with inside information told them it was going to be on that exact coach. Which means Millard, Rooney at the mine, anyone who somehow managed to see a copy of the schedule, or someone at the bank.' Jonah sipped his beer. 'I'll start taking a look for those bandits. After all, it was one of them who raped Louise, which bothers me more than a payroll. But it can wait for tomorrow. How are you at poker?'

'Indifferent. But I play a mean game of cribbage.' Robinson smiled.

'Cribbage it is then.'

Jonah spent the next three days trying to find information on the outlaws. He returned to Animas Forks, then made two fruitless trips to Silverton. On the afternoon of the third day, he left the smoky, noisy saloons and took Jenny out for a buggy ride to relax and catch up properly since his last visit to Motherlode.

Robinson wrote his first letter about Jonah and planned out his feature on Millard. Looking at his notes, he remembered the frequent moves, and out of curiosity, wrote to the editors of newspapers in the towns where Millard had operated, asking for information on his activities in those places.

On returning from his buggy ride, Jonah suggested that they spruce themselves up and went to visit Jenny and her girls. After three days of solitude with his notes and pen, Robinson was happy to agree to the charms of Jenny's parlour house.

There were a couple of other customers there already when they arrived. A buzz of light conversation and laughter filled the air, the sound mingling with the smell of good food from the kitchen. With the lovely women, and the rich fabrics in their dresses and the furnishings, the whole experience was a pleasure for all the senses. Robinson felt more at home this time, greeting

Jenny politely as they joined her in the parlour. All the same, he observed Jonah's confidence with a degree of mild envy when his friend took both of Miss Jenny's hands as he greeted her in turn.

'I'm sorry we've no real news on finding the scum who attacked Miss Louise,' Jonah apologised. He'd purposely avoided the subject during their buggy ride.

Jenny smiled. 'It's good of both of you to take the trouble.'

'It's no trouble,' Jonah reassured her, releasing her hands. 'You know I can't resist a damsel in distress.'

'Is that, can't resist helping her, or can't resist flirting with her?' Jenny asked, making both men laugh.

'Both,' Jonah admitted honestly.

As he spoke, they heard the front door open, and Albert greeting another visitor in the hall. Jenny excused herself, and went to greet the new arrival.

'Why hello, Jonah. I ain't seen you in a long time.' A pretty, blonde girl with a sweet, heart-shaped face approached them.

'Why, Miss Maybelline, you're looking swell,' Jonah replied, smiling. He introduced Robinson, who bowed politely.

Maybelline smiled at the newspaperman. 'I hope you don't mind, sir, but I've been longing to talk to Jonah, here.'

'I came here to do more than just talk,' Jonah said, raising an eyebrow.

'Go ahead,' Robinson said, gesturing at the chairs around the room. 'I rather wanted to see if Miss Sandy was available.'

Jonah wished him good luck, and let himself be towed toward a two-seater sofa by Maybelline. Robinson went the other way, back towards the hall to get to the other parlour. At the doorway, he came face to face with Millard.

'Ah ... er, good evening, yeah?' Robinson greeted the owner of the stagecoach line. For once, he didn't know what to say.

Miss Jenny joined them. 'Charles is a valued guest here,' she said, with a slight stiffness in her tone.

'Of course,' Robinson replied immediately. 'I quite understand that everything that happens here in your house is behind closed doors. You have my word on that.' He looked at Millard as he said the last part.

Millard relaxed, his face switching from thuggish to genial. 'I know you must be thinking of my wife. She is most precious to me.' He unconsciously touched the diamond tiepin he wore as he spoke. 'But I like to spare her the burden of fulfilling my needs as a man. She has done her duty very well as a wife, and given me our four lovely daughters, but I don't wish to trouble her for more than the ordinary amount of . . . affection, that a husband should share with his wife.'

Robinson nodded. 'I can see that.'

Millard apparently took the neutral statement as approval, for he smiled and nodded, before moving past Robinson and into the parlour.

Jenny cast a glance after him and then back at Robinson. She spoke softly. 'Don't feel sorry for his wife; she knows perfectly well where he is. She's quite happy for us to "deal with his urges" but she keeps him on a tight leash. The girls say he's polite and considerate with them, so it all works out rather well.'

She patted Robinson on the arm. 'Go and enjoy yourself.'

Robinson nodded and with Miss Sandy's company, did indeed enjoy himself.

CHAPTER SIX

The house was quiet when Millard returned late that night. He shed his coat and hat quietly, anxious not to disturb his daughters, who were up in their bedrooms and hopefully asleep. The parlour was only lit by one lamp now, the warm light glittering on the jewelry his wife wore.

'Good evening, Mary,' Millard crossed to his wife's chair.

She lowered her needles, the fine white lace she was knitting coiled in her lap.

'Are you satisfied now?' she enquired, looking at him steadily.

'Only in the basest, physical sense, my love,' he said honestly. 'You know there's no other woman could mean as much to me as my wife, the mother of my children, my darling Mary.' He took a small box from his jacket pocket and handed it to her.

Mary took out the gold bar brooch: it was etched

67

with a delicate picture of mountains, and had a small garnet set at either end.

'That's charming,' she said with a smile, and offered her cheek for a kiss.

Millard took the chance to rest his hand briefly on her shoulder as he bent for the kiss: Mary didn't like being touched on the nights he'd been with prostitutes, but tonight she allowed the brief gesture. He sat opposite her and watched as she took up her knitting again.

'Opal was correct when she said she'd never meet a suitable husband here,' Mary said, her needles moving steadily as she talked. 'She needs to be somewhere like Denver, where the big money is.'

'I've only just got the business going here,' Millard reminded her. 'You know we can't make the same kind of success around the big cities. We need to be out where the communications aren't so good. It takes a particular set of circumstances to make money in the way I have been doing.'

'The stage line is your business,' Mary said. 'But the family is mine. What's the point in earning money if it's not being used for the right things? The future of our family is what's important. We have to give our daughters the best advantages we can. You don't want them to end up like the women you were visiting this evening, do you?'

'Of course not!' Millard protested. He swallowed, horrified at the idea his wife had suggested.

'But the business needs to be out here,' he repeated.

'I'll write my youngest sister,' Mary said after a few moments. 'She can come out and keep house for you while I escort Opal for a month's visit to Denver.'

'A month without you?' Millard queried.

Mary nodded firmly. 'At least. It'll take time to get invitations from the right people, and then she can stay with acquaintances at intervals while she's courting. She'll need new clothes when we get to Denver and see what's in style, and we'll have to stay at a decent hotel.'

'You know best, my dear,' Millard said. 'But it's going to be expensive.'

'Once Opal is married, you won't need to keep her,' Mary pointed out. 'You want to walk your daughter down the aisle, don't you?' she added with a gentle smile.

Millard nodded, thinking how handsome Opal would look on her wedding day.

'And once Opal has connections in the right places, it will be simpler and cheaper for the others to find husbands,' Mary added practically.

'You're right,' Millard said again, and leaned back in his armchair to daydream about his daughters in white lace and diamonds, while his wife continued to knit lace.

*

The next morning, Robinson stayed in his hotel room, working on his first letter about Millard for the *New-York Tribune*. He worked at his dressing table, his brush, hair-oil and other sundries pushed aside to make space for his writing slope and the blotting paper and ink set ready to hand. By the late morning, the letter was done and ready in its envelope, and he'd roughed out his next correspondence to the *Rhode Island Chronicle* as well. Putting his rather blunt pencil neatly back in its slot at the top of the leather-fronted slope, Robinson wriggled his fingers and stretched mightily, till the joints in his back popped.

A glance at the window showed him that the earlier cloud had cleared away and it was a bright, fall day outside. Robinson stood, grabbed his jacket and the letter, and paused for a quick glance in the mirror. Remembering Jonah's groomed appearance, he applied a little more hair oil and attempted to brush his curls into something neater. Not entirely satisfied with the result, he put his hat on, put the letter in his pocket and headed outside.

At the post office, Robinson posted his letter and was pleased to find one waiting for him from the editor, with a cheque enclosed for previous work, as well as replies from two of the editors he'd written to about Millard's earlier businesses. Whistling cheerfully, he crossed Panhandle Street and walked down to the bank at the other end. He just reached it when the door opened and Miss Sandy stepped out. He didn't recognize her for a moment, as she was respectably dressed, with full skirts and a matching blue jacket over her white blouse, and her dark-blonde hair covered with a jaunty straw hat.

'Good morning.' She greeted him cheerfully with a bright smile.

Robinson returned the greeting as he raised his hat to her, a gesture that made her smile widen further in delight. 'It's a splendid day, yeah?' he added.

Sandy nodded. 'I was planning to go for a short ride to enjoy the fresh air. It would be more fun to have company, if you're free – unless you have business here?' she added, indicating the bank.

'Nothing that can't wait until this afternoon,' Robinson said impulsively. He didn't do much riding, but Sandy was good company and he'd been in town for a few days now without seeing anywhere new. Robinson was always most curious about other people, their lives and motivations, and he was intrigued by the women at Jenny's place. He turned and began walking back up the street with Sandy by his side.

'Jonah told me that you all have banking accounts,' he remarked.

'Jenny insists,' Sandy told him. 'She doesn't tell

71

us how much to save, or how often, but most of us put something aside each week. It's not a job you can earn at for many years, not good money, anyway,' she added, in a more serious tone than Robinson had previously heard from her. 'I don't want to end up like those women in the cribs,' she said, referring to the rough shacks on the outskirts of town that the cheapest whores lived and worked from. 'Most of them drink or take laudanum to get through; they need it to help, and it doesn't, really.'

'What about playing in the music-halls?' Robinson asked. 'Jonah says you're good enough to sing on stage, yeah?'

Sandy's face lit up again. 'I do love music,' she admitted. 'But I don't care for moving from place to place so often and living out of cheap hotels.'

They continued talking as they returned to the parlour house and the stables there. Sandy had distinct opinions on how she valued her independence and on the double standards applied to women. Talk on women's suffrage occupied Robinson's attention as they left town and rode south along the valley. The conversation was so engrossing that Robinson barely noticed when Sandy increased their pace to a jog, and found himself following her into a gentle lope. He wasn't sorry though when Sandy slowed them back to walk after a while.

'Shakes the liver up, doesn't it, yeah?' he said, slightly out of breath.

She nodded. 'Let's explore up here.' Without waiting for an answer, Sandy turned her roan into a steep sided valley that led up to a wall of towering mountains just a few miles ahead.

Robinson pointed at the snowy peaks that glittered in the clear, bright air. 'That's the Continental Divide, yeah?'

'I think so.' Sandy laughed. 'Don't worry, I don't want to climb up there. I'm more interested in what might be along here.' She turned her attention to the forested slopes either side at the mouth of the gulch.

'What are you looking for? A bird?'

Sandy halted her horse and looked at him with a mix of mischief and defiance that immediately intrigued the newspaperman. 'Jonah thinks that the bandits won't go too far from the area they know, and that they'll have a hideout someplace.' She gestured to the thick trees. 'I reckoned we should go have a look for them.'

'Why here?'

'Plenty of cover; it's as good as anywhere to start looking.'

Robinson grinned. 'All right.' He started his horse forward but almost immediately pulled up again. 'We're looking for bandits, but we're not armed, yeah?'

'I was only going to scout for signs,' Sandy reassured him. 'I don't aim to try arresting them; we can let Jonah take charge of that.'

Robinson nodded, and they started forward again.

This time there was little conversation as they rode. Instead, their attention was on their surroundings, particularly the trees to either side. First Sandy, and then Robinson spotted what seemed to be small paths, but both faded away into nothing. By this time, they had meandered nearly a mile up the gulch, and it was past noon.

'We're almost through the trees,' Robinson said, looking at the steep, grassy slopes leading to the head of the gulch.

Sandy also turned her gaze further up the gulch, and looked disappointed. 'There are other valleys to search.' She sounded as determined as she had before.

'Tomorrow, yeah?' said Robinson, who was hungry and wanted to get back to Motherlode for some lunch. He was also conscious that he was riding Jenny's personal mount, a rangy bay that was almost tall enough to suit him, and didn't want to risk getting it injured.

Sandy just nodded, already turning her horse towards a gap in the trees. She rode in a little way, and bent over to look at the ground. She leaned a little closer, then sat up and beckoned to

Robinson. 'Hoofprints!' she hissed.

Robinson immediately forgot his hunger as he joined her amongst the trees, careful to steer his mount away from the patch of ground that Sandy was looking at. Sure enough, there were two or three faint hoofmarks in the soil. He urged his horse on a few more steps, pointing out a squashed wintergreen plant that looked to have been trodden on. Together, they excitedly worked their way deeper into the trees, finding a faint trail.

'Isn't this fun?' Sandy's face was bright with life as she peered around.

Thinking about what they were doing, rather than simply doing it, made Robinson recall exactly why they had started following this trail. He halted his horse abruptly.

'Hadn't we better be more cautious, yeah? If the bandits are further along this trail, we don't want to come across them precipitately.'

'My,' exclaimed Sandy. 'You sure know some swell words.' Her mischievous smile took the sting from her joke. She kicked her feet from her stirrups. 'We'd better go on on foot.'

Dismounting, they led their horses as they went carefully on. Just a couple of minutes later, they saw a brighter area among the trees ahead.

'It's a clearing; let's take a closer look,' Sandy whispered.

Hitching the horses to trees, they advanced

slowly, keeping to the denser undergrowth where possible. Sure enough, there was a clearing with a small shack and a stable partially visible behind it. Both looked as though they'd been through a couple of hard winters, the tar paper that covered the outsides being torn in several places. The shack door was crudely made from weathered planks, and the small window was half dirty glass, half thin hide.

'Look, smoke,' Sandy pointed to the tinpot chimney. 'If someone's inside, we might be able to hear what they're saying. Wait here.' With a quick grin, she slipped away before Robinson could stop her.

Crouching behind a bristly currant bush, Robinson held his breath as Miss Sandy ran lightly across the grass. She approached the nearer end of the shack, where she couldn't be seen from inside, and pressed herself against the wall to listen. After a few moments, she grinned and nodded at Robinson, then began to walk cautiously around to the front. Robinson had to fight down the urge to call out to her, to tell her to come back. Sandy crept along to the door, placing her feet carefully, and slowly bent towards it to listen at the crack. After just a moment, she jerked back quickly, and Robinson gasped at the sudden movement. The door was flung wide open as an untidily-dressed man came out to fling a dishpan of dirty water across the grass. Sandy turned in an instant and began sprinting back to the safety of the trees. Robinson bobbed about, unsure whether to leave cover and try to help.

'What, hey!' The man dropped the dishpan and sprinted after Sandy, catching her in a couple of strides. Grabbing her arm, he whirled her round. Sandy immediately boxed his ear.

'Unhand me at once!' she yelled imperiously.

'Hell, no.' The man grinned as he seized her free arm and pinned them together.

Just as Robinson decided he must do something, two more men spilled out of the shack.

'Look what I found!' the first man crowed, turning so they could see Sandy, struggling in his grip.

The two men bounded across; one whistled in appreciation.

'Say, that's one purty piece you got there, Chip. Are there any more like you round here?' he asked.

'No,' Sandy replied firmly. Not once did she glance towards Robinson's position. 'I came out here on my own to get away from the other girls for a while.'

'Other girls?' the one holding Sandy said. 'She's gotta be a saloon girl or a whore; there ain't nowhere else you find a bunch of women cooped up together.'

'Them smart clothes means she a good one, too.' A man with thinning, red hair reached out to pat Sandy's bosom.

'You might not fancy company but we ain't had no company for a whiles,' the first man said, breathing into Sandy's ear. 'Especially not nothing so purty as you. You're coming in to spend some time with us.'

'After you came all this way out of town and right to our place, it'd be downright rude not to invite you-all in, now wouldn't it?' the red-haired one said. He flourished an elaborate bow and gestured to the door. 'After you, miss.'

'It's Miss Sandy,' Sandy said calmly. She ceased wriggling. 'These clothes were expensive, and I'll thank you not to pull them around. Very well, I accept your kind invitation.'

Although the first man kept hold of her arms, Sandy managed to give the appearance of leading him as she entered the shabby shack with the men. As the door closed behind them, Robinson backed away, pausing briefly to untangle his jacket from the spines of the currant bush. What was he going to do now?

CHAPTER SEVEN

Robinson stayed frozen in place until the door closed. Then the spell broke and he gasped in a deep breath. Help: he had to get help. Backing through the undergrowth, he tore his trousers and scratched the back of his hand, but barely noticed. Once clear, he jogged back to the horses, thankfully still where they'd been left.

'We've got to make haste now, yeah?' he said to his borrowed horse as he unfastened the reins. Robinson dismissed the idea of taking Sandy's horse with him. It was too far for Sandy to have walked from town, so if the outlaws went looking for her horse and didn't find it, they would probably guess correctly that another person had taken it away. Turning his own horse, Robinson found himself looking blankly into the trees for a few moments. Picking out the faint trail they'd followed would take time. Jonah wouldn't sit dithering; what would he do?

Thinking about his surroundings as landscape, Robinson got his answer. All he had to do was to keep moving downhill, and he would reach the creek in the middle of the gulch, which would lead him back down to the river valley. His face lit up, and he set the rangy horse in motion, ducking to scrape beneath the trees.

By the time they reached Motherlode, Robinson was more out of breath than his horse. He wasn't too unhappy to slow to a jog to pass between a crowd of laden burros and a wagon. Breathing heavily, he looked about, trying to guess where Jonah might be. Looking up and down the busy street, Robinson wondered where to begin. He tried to check his horse, but the bay was striding out keenly and shook its head. Robinson realized it was aiming for its stable, and food. Searching in the town for Jonah would be easier on foot than on horseback, so Robinson let the bay make its way between buildings and into the yard behind Jenny's parlour house.

Robinson slid gratefully, if not gracefully, from the saddle and tied the horse to a ring on the stable wall. 'Someone will take care of you, yeah?' he told it, patting it on the neck before heading across the yard.

The rear door of the parlour house led directly into the kitchen. At the table was a tallish, fair man wearing a cook's apron, and the black doorman,

Albert, drinking coffee together.

'Ah, good afternoon,' Robinson said. 'I was out with Miss Sandy; she assured me it was acceptable for me to borrow Miss Jenny's horse.' His brain began to catch up with his actions. 'Is Miss Jenny in? I need to see her on a rather urgent matter.'

'She's in her office with Mr. Durrell,' Albert informed him.

'Oh, excellent! I was hoping she might know where Jonah is, yeah? I need him to help Miss Sandy.'

'Help Miss Sandy?' Albert repeated, coming to his feet, fast.

Robinson nodded. 'It is rather urgent.'

Albert led him through to the front of the house, and to Jenny's office, behind the music parlour. He knocked once before opening the door.

'Miss Jenny? Mr. Robinson here says Miss Sandy needs help.'

Jonah stood up as Robinson entered the room. 'What's this about Sandy?'

Robinson quickly and clearly explained to them both what had happened.

'I'll go put on riding clothes; Albert, please call Erica,' Jenny said, hurrying to the door. She departed, calling for her maid to help her change quickly.

Robinson stared after her, but his attention was

brought back by Jonah asking if he'd recognized any of the bandits.

'Well, no,' Robinson admitted. 'I was too worried about Miss Sandy to look closely at the men apprehending her.'

'All right. What was the shack like? How big was the clearing?' Jonah asked.

'Um. . . . A picture paints a thousand words, yeah?' Robinson took a pencil from Jenny's desk and drew a diagram of the clearing and buildings on some blotting paper. He neatly sketched in the window and door, showing which way it opened.

'We'll need more than three guns,' Jonah mused, studying the diagram.

'Marshal Tapton may bring someone with him,' Robinson suggested.

Jonah shook his head. 'Tapton won't come; it's out of his jurisdiction and he doesn't approve of whores, so he won't go out of his way to help them.' He turned and looked Robinson in the eyes. 'Have you ever used a gun in combat?'

Robinson straightened himself. 'Not often,' he admitted. 'But on my first trip west, I helped to fight off a war party of Comanches that attacked the stagecoach I was travelling in. It was rather stimulating, but also brutal. I killed men, and I saw others killed. I didn't panic under fire,' he added with a touch of pride.

Jonah nodded. 'I'm glad to hear it; so, we'll have

four guns then.'

Robinson frowned. 'You and me; who else?'

Jonah grinned at him. 'Why do you think Jenny and Erica are getting ready to come with us? I've seen them in a gunfight and they don't panic under fire either.' He clapped Robinson on the shoulder. 'Come on, let's get the horses ready.'

They were on their way sooner than Robinson had expected. The women wore simple, practical clothes and rode astride. Jenny was riding one of the chestnut carriage horses she kept, and had her Winchester on her saddle; Erica carried her shotgun. There were an anxious few moments when Robinson struggled to find the place where he and Sandy had turned off and headed into the trees, but Erica spotted the marks they had left and the four were quickly on the move again.

The group spoke very little, conferring now and again over the faint trail. At Robinson's suggestion, they dismounted and began to lead their horses.

'Much further?' Jonah asked.

The newspaperman looked around thoughtfully, squinting into the trees ahead. He absently pushed his springy, brown curls back from his forehead, vaguely aware of his somewhat dishevelled state. Jonah, in contrast, looked nearly as smart as he had at breakfast. Part of Robinson's mind automatically registered the disparity as an interesting note for a letter, but he was more concerned with their current situation.

'I think we're quite close,' he said softly. 'We should leave our horses here.'

The others took his word, hitching their mounts, apart from Jonah, who left his grey horse ground tied. Creeping forward, the clearing soon became visible through the trees. Jonah crouched behind a deadfall that was smothered in mountain snowberry. As they looked, there was a sudden burst of noise, accompanied by a shrill whistle, from inside the shack.

'What are they doing?' whispered Robinson anxiously.

Jenny frowned in puzzlement. 'It sounded rather like applause.'

'Good heavens; they're not applauding one another for. . .' Erica stopped speaking as another sound was heard.

After a few moments, they made out the opening lines of a bawdy song in Sandy's distinctive voice.

Erica stifled a giggle, her eyes shining. 'How clever of her. Sandy's found another way to entertain them until help arrives.'

Jonah nodded in approval. 'Well, help's here now,' he said. 'Jenny, you and I'll go around this side,' he said, gesturing to the left. 'Robinson, you and Erica will approach from the right; they can't see us approaching from the sides, luckily. When we've all reached the shack, we'll get into position along the front. Robinson and Erica, you crouch beneath the window, ready to pop up, break it and cover them when I go in. You'll be after me,' he added to Jenny.

The other three nodded, their expressions sober. Jonah had talked to them on the ride from town, reminding them of the importance of not relaxing their guard, and that a man wasn't out of the fight until disarmed. The pairs separated, making their ways around the edge of the clearing to their appointed positions. Robinson peeked out and saw Jonah opposite. When the manhunter gave the signal, Robinson moved cautiously into the open, his plain revolver in hand. He kept the gun in excellent condition, and practised target shooting every three or four months, but it was years since he'd last held a weapon with the intention of actually fighting with it. His nerves were buzzing as he paced rapidly across the grass to the shack.

Only when he reached the end wall safely, did he glance back. Erica was a couple of steps behind him, a look of cool determination on her lovely face. Reassured by the competent way she carried her shotgun, Robinson turned to see Jonah and Jenny in place at the other end of the building. Jonah nodded and began stepping along the front of the shack to the door. Robinson took a couple of steps towards him, before crouching to make his way beneath the window.

He was hunched awkwardly, his long limbs folded at odd angles as he tried to keep low. Looking up to check where Jonah was, Robinson lost his balance and fell sideways against the front of the shack. He bit off a short yelp of surprise as his shoulder crashed into the thin boards. As Robinson pushed himself back to his feet, a shout from inside cut through Sandy's singing.

'What was. . .? Something hit. . . .'

Jonah wasted no time. Throwing his shoulder against the shack door, he burst inside, guns in hand. Only the speed he was moving saved his life.

As Robinson rose, Erica was smashing the glass at the bottom of the window with the butt of her shotgun. Annoyed with himself, he gave the dirty glass a hearty smack with his revolver, sending shards everywhere.

A bullet cracked past Jonah's shoulder as he dived towards the centre of the shack. He found himself facing three armed men.

'Surrender! Drop your weapons!' he snapped, even as he was assessing what he saw. Sandy had to be behind him, at the other end of the shack. One of the three men in front, a man with thinning, reddish hair, was trying to correct his aim, follow-ing Jonah's fast entry. Jonah's long revolver seemed to aim itself. He fired, and the man twisted, falling before he even got his hand to his gun. Even as he saw his first target drop, Jonah glimpsed movement to one side that warned him of danger. He fired fast with his other gun, but the sound of his shot was drowned out by the boom of a shotgun. Blood sprayed the walls of the shack as another man fell, his torso half-shredded by the close-range shot. The smells of wood-smoke and tobacco were replaced by the sharper ones of gun-powder and blood. The last of the three men, his untidy clothing spattered with blood, hastily raised his hands.

Jonah was about to speak when there was a dull, metallic clang from behind, and a cry of pain.

'It's all right,' came Sandy's voice. 'You don't need to worry about this one.'

Jenny, standing beside Jonah, looked over her shoulder and chuckled. 'I thought you said you were no good with a frying pan?'

'Only for cooking,' Sandy corrected. 'I never said anything about fighting.'

Robinson appeared in the doorway. 'I'm awfully sorry, yeah?'

'Never mind,' Jonah said practically. 'Go help Miss Sandy with her assailant while I cuff this fellow. Then I'll have to see to this pair of fools before we can head back to town with them all.'

While Robinson and Sandy dealt with the man at the other end of the room, Jonah watched the uninjured man unbuckle his gunbelt one handed, and toss it onto a nearby bunk. He made no trouble as Jonah cuffed him; he kept glancing in the direction of the window and Erica's shotgun. Ignoring the red-haired man's pleas for help, Jonah knelt by the one hit by the shotgun. Bright blood bubbled around the man's lips, almost the only sign of life. Jonah felt for the pulse in his neck, finding it thin and fast.

'This may be of some use,' Robinson suggested, bending to offer a greasy blanket.

Jonah spread it over the dying man; dark patches of blood bloomed on the wool almost immediately as it soaked through. He looked at the newspaperman. Robinson's face was compassionate but not shaken as he studied the outlaw.

'Come on,' Jonah said, rising and moving to the red-haired man. 'Help me move this fool, Robinson, then fetch the black bag from my saddle, would you?'

'Of course. I'd love to see your doctor work, yeah?' Robinson answered, his attention immediately diverted by the thought of new material for his letters.

Robinson felt somewhat self-conscious as they all rode back into Motherlode that afternoon, with the three sullen bandits under restraints and a blanket-wrapped body tied across the saddle of the fourth horse. A search of the shack and stable had produced a couple of hundred dollars in bank bags, but nothing else that looked like the proceeds of a robbery. Jonah smiled cheerfully at the spectators, tipping his hat politely to a couple of women outside a grocery store. Robinson wished he'd combed his hair, but consoled himself with the thought that he was the least-striking member of the party, so no one would notice his appearance. As they halted outside the law office, Marshal Tapton came hurrying along the sidewalk.

'What have you been up to now?' he growled at Jonah.

The manhunter slid gracefully from his saddle. 'Miss Sandy and Robinson uncovered a little nest of vipers up Maggie Gulch.'

Tapton studied the red-haired bandit that Jonah had injured. 'That's Rob Roper; he's done a couple of years for rustling, that I know of. What's he been up to now?'

'We were looking for the criminals who robbed the stage and attacked Miss Louise,' said Robinson, joining them. 'Though I must confess that none of them look familiar and they deny having anything to do with the hold-up.'

'Let's get them inside and off of the street,' Tapton ordered.

It didn't take long to get the living bandits locked up and the undertaker sent for to collect the dead one. While Tapton took a statement from

Sandy and Robinson, the others looked through a stack of wanted dodgers taken from a wooden box that did service as a filing cabinet. It didn't take long, as Sandy had charmed the men into giving her their first names as she occupied their attention harmlessly. They were wanted for a variety of simple offences, like rustling or store robberies.

'This lot's near on as useless as tits on a bull,' Jonah remarked. 'I don't reckon they could be involved in what needs real planning like stealing a payroll from a stage.'

'Perhaps if Louise came and saw them?' Erica suggested. 'She'd recognize the one who hurt her, and then we'd have a witness placing them at the scene.'

Marshal Tapton spoke up. 'It'd be her word against his and a jury ain't gonna take a whore's word against a man's.'

'Not even when the man's a wanted criminal?' Sandy asked angrily.

'Whores are criminals too.' Tapton stared flatly at her.

Sandy hissed like an angry snake. Jonah moved smoothly to stand beside her.

'It ain't fair,' he said, his dark eyes flashing but his voice calm. 'But the marshal's right. Some folks won't take a woman's word over a man's, no matter how respectable she is, and there's plenty more who hardly even see prostitutes as people. It's their loss,' he added, looking down into Sandy's face. 'They miss out on getting to know some brave, funny, honest and loyal friends.'

Some of the tension left Sandy's body as she smiled back. 'Thank you.'

'You're welcome. And thanks to you, there's five-hundred dollars of bounty to be collected on these jackasses.' He held the sheaf of wanted notices out to the lawman. 'That divides nicely into one-hundred dollars each.'

'That's the best news I've heard all day!' Sandy exclaimed.

CHAPTER EIGHT

The group returned to Miss Jenny's house, where a meal was quickly prepared for Sandy and Robinson, who had both missed lunch. Coffee and cake was served for everyone as they talked over recent events.

'Well, that was a profitable little diversion,' Jonah said, leaning back in his chair. 'But it gets us no closer to finding the bandits. I feel like I've been to every saloon, pool hall, gambling den, whorehouse and dance hall in Motherlode, Silverton and Animas Forks, but I've heard nothing so far.'

'Now a few days have passed, maybe you should start again at the beginning?' Sandy suggested, and laughed at Jonah's sour expression.

'Maybe they'll go to the dance on Friday night,' Erica suggested light-heartedly.

'A dance?' Jonah cheered up. 'Where?'

Erica shrugged. 'It's in that empty building between the two cafés. It's a respectable do, in order to raise money to start a school.'

'Isn't Mrs. Millard something important in the school committee?' asked Sandy.

Jenny nodded. 'We're good enough to service her husband and take his money, but not good enough to be seen in public at the same events as him, even if we give some of that money back for a good cause.'

'She's a wizened, old hypocrite who wouldn't know how to have a good time if she tripped over it,' Sandy snorted.

'It doesn't sound like the kind of shindig a bunch of owlhoots would go to,' Jonah said. 'Not unless they fix themselves up with some fancy clothes. Most thieves get money and just spend it, but this lot seem to be keeping it close.'

'Maybe they put their money in the bank too?' Sandy suggested drily.

'What about the other things they took?' Erica asked. 'There was a watch, wasn't there, and Louise's brooch?'

'I forgot about that!' Jonah exclaimed. 'She said it was a gift.'

Robinson drew out his notebook and flipped it to the right page. 'I forgot to write a note about it.' He sounded surprised at his omission. 'I guess I was more concerned with the attack on her, so the brooch escaped my attention, yeah?' He looked at the others as though asking forgiveness for his incomplete notes.

'We'll get a description of it from her,' Jonah said. 'So we can look out for it and try to track the outlaws through it. I'll go back to Silverton tomorrow.'

'I need to go back to the bank again,' Sandy said cheerfully. 'I have a hundred dollars to deposit in my account. Or maybe I'll save ninety and spend ten. Didn't you say there were some charming new hats in the drapers?' she asked Erica.

'Oh yes,' Erica replied, smiling. She drained the last of her coffee. 'The bank, the drapers, and the hardware store; I need some more shells for my shotgun.'

Jonah laughed. 'And that sentence is why I love being around you ladies. You make life so interesting!'

Millard tickled Amethyst, making her squeal and wriggle.

'Amethyst, ladies do not shriek like banshees,' Mary admonished. 'They speak quietly.' She gave an accusing look to her husband.

'I'm sorry,' Millard apologized to both. He let go of his youngest daughter. 'Go and sit with Ruby and practise that figuring you were doing.' He watched fondly as she joined her sister. The early evening with his family about him, was his favourite time of the day. Ruby was reading a book about birds, while Mary was showing Opal how to do something complicated with white thread and a small shuttle, while Pearl watched.

Pearl looked up from her mother's lesson. 'Papa? What happened in town this afternoon? I heard some bad men had been caught.'

'Yes, I believe that manhunter, Jonah Durrell, found a gang of outlaws who were living somewhere close to town,' Millard replied. 'They're all in jail now, so there's nothing to worry about.'

'I've seen that manhunter,' Opal interrupted, her eyes wide. 'He's a very, very handsome man. So dreamy looking.' She gave a little sigh.

'Never marry a man because of how he looks,' Mary said. 'A sound income is far more important in a husband. Raising a family well is an expensive business.' She looked up at her own husband. 'This Durrell seems to be successful at what he does. Is he looking for the men who robbed your stagecoach?'

'I believe he is, my dear.'

Mary thought for a few moments, the tatting shuttle idle in her hands. 'Handsome men like him are often very vain. I'm surprised he does something as rough as chasing criminals when there's a risk he could get scarred in a fight. Still, I'm sure he knows the risks,' she added, giving her husband a piercing look.

Millard nodded. 'I'm sure he takes care of himself. Is dinner ready yet?'

Mary glanced at the clock. 'In a few minutes, dear.'

Millard took himself to his favourite chair and sat down, watching as his wife continued with the tatting lesson.

Jonah's enquiries in Silverton finally produced a rumour of a man bragging about how he'd got a 'free taste of one of them fancy doves from Motherlode'.

'It was up in Gladstone,' Jonah told Jenny and three of her girls as they sat in the private parlour late that afternoon. 'I'll take a ride up there tomorrow.'

'Can I go with you?' asked Miss Megan.

Jonah turned in surprise to Megan, who was combing out her waist-length flaxen hair. She looked straight back at him with honest, blue eyes that held a hint of mischief.

'I missed out on the fun when you rescued Sandy,' she explained. 'And I want to feel that I'm doing something useful towards catching the scum that attacked you, Louise.'

'I sure do appreciate all you're doing,' Louise said. 'But I'm minded to think I don't care too hard any more about finding him. Sure, if you hog-tie him and give him to me, I'd stamp on his face and his balls, but you're all taking so much trouble. I can forget it and move on.'

'My job is to find bad people and see they get punished,' Jonah said. 'If your attacker goes behind bars, he won't be able to hurt another woman, maybe one who doesn't have your grit. That's enough motivation for me.'

Louise nodded. 'I see.' She gave a short sigh. 'I guess I'm all right with that. Prevent them from hurting other folk,' she said, mulling the idea over.

Jonah turned to Megan. 'Gladstone's nothing more than a big mining camp. It's just boarding houses, saloons and a store.'

'And I bet there's hardly a woman there,' she replied. 'A few in the saloons, I guess, but no parlour house women.' Megan grinned. 'It's sure astonishing what the sight of some frills and lace can do to a lonely man. I bet I'll find them quite willing to help poor, little old me.' She lowered her head a little to look up at Jonah, suddenly appearing more submissive and helpless.

He smiled in surprise at how effective the gesture was. 'I guess you might learn something,' he admitted. 'But don't stray too far from me. If this son-of-a-bitch is around Gladstone, you don't want to give him the chance to get hold of you too.'

Megan nodded, dropping the helpless pose. 'I'll be careful,' she promised.

97

When she met Jonah at the livery barn the next morning, Megan was wearing a stylish but modest walking outfit, with her flaxen hair pinned up neatly beneath a straw boater. Jonah helped her into the hired buggy and they set off north towards Gladstone. It was a nice distance away, a pleasant drive that allowed for a comfortable amount of conversation. As Jonah had said, Gladstone was just a large mining camp, far less developed than Motherlode. He halted the buggy outside the general store, hitching the horse before giving Miss Megan a hand as she descended. Already, men in the busy street were stopping to look at her. Megan looked around in return, smiling sweetly.

'This looks like being interesting,' she commented quietly to Jonah.

He looked around cautiously, noting a small group of men who already seemed to be having a discussion about the young woman.

'We'd best take things carefully,' Jonah told her.

A gaudily-dressed saloon girl stuck her head out of a door, stared coldly at Megan, then tossed her head and retreated inside.

'You should be all right in here,' Jonah said, indicating the store.

Megan nodded. 'It's just nice to see someplace other than Motherlode now and again. I've only been to Silverton twice. There's new places being settled all the time, the whole of the west's opening up and changing, but once a working girl gets to a new town, she doesn't see much of anything outside of her brothel.'

Turning, Jonah noticed one of the men nearby being pushed forward by the others. He waited quietly, balanced and alert as the miner approached Megan. She faced the man with a pleasant smile as he stopped in front of her and removed his dusty hat.

'Excuse me, Miss,' he said, twirling his hat in his broad hands. 'You're one of the church ladies, ain't you?'

Megan blinked, then a smile blossomed on her face. 'Why, yes, I am.'

The miner turned to his group of friends and beckoned to them. 'We're plumb glad to hear that,' he said to Megan with simple sincerity. 'There ain't no church close enough for us to visit and I sure do miss hearing the good word spoken.'

'I'm sorry to hear that,' Megan said gently.

The rest of his group had joined them, and others were stopping to watch. Jonah listened with interest to the conversation as he continued to scan their surroundings.

'It's swell of you to come among us,' one of the older men said to Megan.

'It sure is a refreshment to see a decent young woman like you in a place like this,' one of the others added. 'Men got to have entertainment, but without the balance of good folk and proper habits, it's sure easy to fall into the ways of sin and excess.'

'I'm glad to hear you feel that way,' Megan said with an admirably straight face. 'Your attitude does you credit.'

A wiry man limped forward a pace and held out a small, soft-backed book. 'Please, Miss. My ma gave me this Bible when I left home but I don't read too good. I ain't seen a church in months and it would sure be a delight iffen you were to read some passages from the Bible.'

Some of the gathering crowd spoke up in support of the idea, pleading for a Bible reading from the lady. Megan paused a moment, then took the book from him.

'Women are forbidden to preach, but I'll read the Bible for you if you wish.' She looked at Jonah, then glanced along the street at the saloons before returning her gaze to the manhunter.

Jonah nodded. 'I'm sure you'll be fine here with these gentlemen.'

Megan thought for a moment, then started turning the pages. 'The gospel of Saint Luke,' she announced, and began reading the passage of the anointing of Jesus by the repentant prostitute.

Jonah swallowed a laugh, and took advantage of the moment to leave and start visiting the saloons to look for the outlaws.

Some two hours later, they were on their way

back to Motherlode. Once they were well out of Gladstone, Megan asked Jonah if he'd learned anything about the outlaws.

'Well, you know it ain't an easy job asking questions about folks. It takes experience to find the right people to talk to, but I'm very good at what I do, you know,' he said gravely.

'You flirted with a saloon girl, didn't you?' Megan said astutely.

Jonah grinned. 'Works like a charm. I'm not just a pretty face, but having one can sure make things easier sometimes.'

'Shame on you for taking advantage like that,' she said, mock-serious.

'Now who's the pot calling the kettle black? Anyhow,' he went on, 'Mary-Lou told me about this group that comes in once a week or so. She remembered them particularly because one of them paid her a compliment, and another said she wasn't anything special and couldn't compare to the fancy whore from Motherlode he'd had a couple of weeks back. He said he didn't care if they were in the middle of a job, he wasn't passing up the chance to have one like that redhead, for free.'

'That must have been Louise!' Megan exclaimed.

Jonah nodded. 'One of the others told him to shut up, pretty fast, and called him Brewster. Mary-Lou remembered because it was Brewster who insulted her.'

'Serve him right if he gets caught because she remembers his name.'

'There's five of them. Mary-Lou said they weren't miners: she thought they might be cowhands, but they haven't bragged about the brand they ride for. They don't mix much and they don't spend too much. They have enough for meals, drinks and gambling, without counting the pennies, but they're not throwing dollars around. I've got Brewster's name now, and some description of the others. I'll call on the marshal when we get back and talk to him. And what about you? Did you have an interesting time?' He raised an eyebrow.

Megan assumed a demure expression and looked back at him. They stared at one another for a few moments, before Jonah was the first to crack and burst out laughing. Megan laughed too, giggling in the corner of the lazy-back seat.

'Shame on you,' Jonah said. 'Pretending to be a respectable church lady.'

'The men made that mistake,' Megan protested. 'They were hoping for a nice church lady and I didn't like to disappoint them.'

'That's Jenny's motto, isn't it? My ladies will never disappoint you.'

This brought another attack of laughter. Megan recovered first; she fished in the pocket of her skirt and produced a small, heavy purse.

'They did more than listen,' she said. 'They gave me this money towards the church they thought I was collecting for. I couldn't refuse it by that stage.'

'Well, you earned it. What will you do with it?'

'Oh, I can't keep it,' Megan said immediately. 'It was given in charity. I don't think anyone's aiming to raise a church in Motherlode yet, but I guess I could give it to the school fund instead.'

'That would be an honourable thing to do,' Jonah approved. He grinned. 'I swear, I never thought you knew the Bible like that.'

'There was nothing else to do on Sunday except read the Bible.'

They compared their childhood experiences of Sundays as the buggy followed the trail up a steep-sided gulch south of Gladstone. The gunshot took them completely by surprise.

CHAPTER NINE

One of the buggy horses reared, the other bolted forwards. Megan was thrown into the side of the swaying buggy, while Jonah braced himself with his feet against the dashboard and gathered up the loosened reins. He swore as three men galloped out from the trees, guns in hand. Fighting to control the panicked horses, Jonah couldn't reach for his own guns. Megan clung to the side of the buggy with one hand and pulled at his coat with the other, trying to reach his holster. One of the approaching men went to the buggy horses while the other two approached either side. All three had revolvers aimed at the pair on the seat.

'Leave it,' Jonah hissed to Megan. 'Too risky.'

She sat back, deliberately straightening her hat as the buggy horses were brought under control by the joint efforts of Jonah and the mounted man.

The other two came alongside the buggy, guns

fixed on the travellers. The one nearest Jonah was a heavyset man with a broad, Slavic face.

'You, down.' The ambusher grabbed Jonah's arm and hauled him from the seat.

Jonah managed to toss the reins in Megan's direction as he fell from the buggy. He landed on his feet, but heavily and off-balance. The rider had slipped his feet from his stirrups: he gave Jonah a sound kick that sent him staggering, and dismounted fast. Jonah had just caught his balance when he was seized, spun and shoved again. Half-dizzied, he glimpsed the heavy man holstering his gun and producing a large knife. The bright blade stuck a sudden fear deep into Jonah's body. He froze for a moment, eyes on the blade, before trying to dodge away. His attacker was already closing on him. A heavy blow to the stomach took Jonah's breath, and the next thing he knew, he was pinned against the side of the buggy, with that large blade against his face.

Jonah held absolutely still, hardly even breathing. He was vaguely aware of the buggy in front of him, but it was the blade at the corner of his eye that held his attention. The knife wasn't quite touching him, but the skin from his eye to his jaw tingled in anticipation of it.

'You've been asking questions about the stage that was robbed,' growled the heavyset man in a thick accent. 'That ain't none of yer business. This is just a warning, see? Forget about the stage. Move on from Motherlode for a while. Go chase someone who's killed someone.' There was the lightest of touches against his face from the blade. Jonah held himself rigid, fighting down the urge to shudder. After some long, long moments, the blade lifted slightly again.

'You know what this knife could do to your face, don't you?' came the voice. 'It wouldn't take much for a sharp knife to open up right to the bone. A lovely, long scar you could have, right where all the women couldn't miss it. Or maybe just trim your nose a little bit, take the tip off of it. If you didn't learn your lesson the first time, next time you could lose an eye. You sure wouldn't look so swell with one eye gone. Geddit?'

'Yes,' Jonah whispered.

'Good.' There was a rumbling chuckle with the word. 'Drake! Come tie him up.'

The knife stayed close to Jonah's face as another man came and tied his wrists behind his back. Jonah was still held against the buggy as the knife was finally moved away.

'The girl can get you out of those ties afore long. They're just so as you cain't shoot at us as we leave. This is the friendly warning, remember? If I was feeling mean, I'd take them fancy guns off of you.'

'I'm sure grateful,' Jonah said sourly.

There was another rumbling chuckle. 'Stay like

that till we're clear,' he ordered.

Jonah stayed facing the buggy as the heavy man mounted and the trio rode away. He remained silent as Megan tugged at the knots in the rope. When his hands were free, he thanked her and helped her back up into the buggy before climbing up himself.

'Sorry,' he said, as he started the horses moving again. 'I should have been paying more attention. It was plumb stupid of me.'

'You didn't ask them to come and threaten you,' Megan replied. She looked thoughtfully at him. 'Are you all right?'

Jonah just nodded. 'Let's get back to town.'

Megan didn't ask any more questions, but sat quietly as the horses trotted up the trail.

Jonah felt a little bad about not keeping up a conversation, but he really didn't want to talk at that moment. He was still tensed up inside with a confusing mix of feelings. Anger was easy to identify; he'd always hated bullies and threatening thugs were merely bullies to him. There was something else, something . . . shameful. Was that it: shame? It wasn't that he'd been ambushed, though it hurt his professional pride. As he thought back, the memory of the knife, so close to his face, brought on the shudders he'd repressed at the time. There was a sick feeling of fear in his stomach that surprised him.

Jonah took a deep breath and turned his attention outwards for a minute, taking in the open mountain scenery and the sunshine, warm on his face. He loved this clean, fresh country, and the endless views and as so often, it helped him to relax. As he looked at the clouds moving overhead, he pondered on his vanity. The threat of the knife against his face had scared him more than any other moment in his life. It wasn't the first time someone had threatened his looks, but before, it had always been fist fights. He'd had a couple of black eyes, bruises and a split lip, but none of it had scared him as much as the threat of deliberate cutting with the knife.

To be scarred, no longer the handsome man that turned heads, that was a difficult idea for Jonah. He had always joked about his vanity, but he was surprised to find how deep it really ran. Jonah thought about the threat. He didn't want to give in to whoever wanted him to quit this manhunt. He didn't want to have his face cut up either but simple vanity, no matter how deep, was no reason to be a coward. And that's what he'd be if he gave in.

Back in Motherlode, Jonah said farewell to Megan, returned the buggy to the livery stable, and headed to Marshal Tapton's office. Although the September day was mild, the marshal had a small fire lit in his heater. He looked up from writing in his log book as Jonah entered.

'Don't take up law work,' the marshal said. 'I just spent half an hour sorting a dispute between two saloons about who was dumping trash in whose yard.' With that, he went back to his slow writing.

Jonah passed the time by first writing some details of the ambush in his small notepad. Tucking notepad and pencil back into the pocket of his waistcoat, he started rummaging through the wanted posters. When Tapton gave a sigh of relief that fluttered the ends of his moustache, and closed the log book, Jonah brought two posters over and put them on the desk. The marshal gave him a stare that said he was being most inconvenient, but looked them over anyway.

'Eli Brewster and George Wilde. Thieving, rustling, horse stealing and robbery,' he said. 'Were busy around Boulder a few years back and Wilde was identified for certain sure at a robbery in Florence a couple of years back. I ain't heard mention of them round here.' Tapton looked at Jonah thoughtfully. 'You got a general interest in them or you reckon they're involved in that stagecoach robbery?'

Jonah nodded. 'These two and a couple of others have been hanging about Gladstone recently: Brewster's been bragging on how he assaulted Miss Louise.'

'What about the payroll?' Tapton asked. 'That

was worth a darn sight more than what passes for that fancy whore's virtue.'

Jonah bit back his first reply. 'No sign of them flashing money about,' he said. 'But there's someone serious about that money not being found.' He described the ambush, and the heavy-set man who'd threatened him.

Tapton grunted. 'That'll be Russian Peter. He's been around town a few months. Does casual work here and there – anything that needs muscle more than brains. Has a side-line in debt-collecting. He shows up, flexes his muscles and reminds people they need to pay up.'

'And I guess they usually do,' Jonah said, remembering the sheer size of the man.

'He doesn't often need to hit anyone, but when he does, he hits them from hell to breakfast.'

'Does he ever get arrested for it?' Jonah asked, raising an eyebrow.

'He's not robbing anyone, just taking what's owed,' the marshal pointed out. 'He don't go too far; he's smart enough for that. I've locked him up a couple of nights when he's had a hideful of rotgut,' he added.

Jonah nodded. 'So, if someone's paid him to put a scare into me, it's a fair bet it's someone local who doesn't want me making enquiries into the robbery.'

'Seems likely,' Tapton agreed. He thought for a

moment. 'Brewster and his gang aren't locals, so far as I know. And iffen they robbed the stage, then why aren't they telling you to butt out for themselves?'

'I don't know,' Jonah admitted. He picked up the wanted dodgers. 'Mind if I borrow these a couple of days?'

'Suit yourself.'

Jonah folded the papers neatly and tucked them in the pocket of his frock coat. Thanking the marshal for his help, he left the office and made his way back to his hotel.

Robinson stared at his reflection in the mirror, twisting slightly from side to side to see how the light moved across the peacock-blue satin of his new vest. It was a bolder colour than he usually wore, but Jonah had suggested it and there was no doubt that the manhunter had style. Robinson felt uncommonly satisfied with his appearance; he relaxed and smiled, which was more charming than the new clothes or tidy hair. The satisfaction lasted until he met up with Jonah in the lobby of their hotel.

'You look swell,' Jonah said warmly.

'I believed I did until I saw you just now,' Robinson replied ruefully.

Jonah offered a wry smile. 'Handsome is as handsome does. I won't look like this forever.'

111

'Everyone gets old, yeah?' Robinson said. 'Unless they die prematurely, and being alive is surely better than dying, even with grey hair, and lines on your face.'

'I guess so,' Jonah said thoughtfully. 'In either case, I guess it's best to make the most of being young and handsome. Come on.' He led the way out.

Unsurprisingly, when they entered the temporary dance hall, it was Jonah who drew the attention. Robinson watched with some amusement as women preened themselves and shuffled around, trying to draw attention without looking too obvious, and various men stood straighter and scowled at the manhunter. They had entered as a dance finished and there was a pause as people mingled and returned to friends or took drinks. Jonah looked around with interest, fully aware of the attention he was drawing. It pleased him, as always, but he was more conscious of it somehow. He tried to imagine the reaction if his face were disfigured by Russian Peter and felt a kind of cold nausea. Taking a deep breath, Jonah put the thought to the back of his mind and switched his attention to the present.

The next dance was soon announced, and Jonah looked around again. There was an immediate rustling among the younger women present as they discreetly jostled for position. Robinson's eye was drawn to the lamplight sparkling on the jewelry worn by Millard's wife and the two daughters with him. All three women wore earrings, brooches and rings that glittered with jewels. The statuesque girl giggled and waved coyly in Jonah's direction; the slender one tossed her brown ringlets and fidgeted with her fan. Jonah flashed a quick smile in their direction, then looked around a moment more before making his choice. The young woman he approached wore a modest dress of dark-green, trimmed with cream lace. She wore no jewelry, only a ribbon topknot in her light-brown hair, and she was one of the plainest women Robinson had ever seen.

Her eyes widened as Jonah approached and asked her to dance. As he took her arm and led her onto the floor, she gazed at him with wonder, and a dawning look of happiness. Robinson smiled as he watched them. As the dance floor began to fill up, he looked around and realized that every woman present had been claimed for a dance. As was common on the frontier, the men outnumbered the women, and Robinson had been too engrossed in watching his friend, to get a partner himself while he had the chance. With a mental shrug, he headed for the bar.

An hour later, Robinson found himself talking to the Millards between dances. He'd managed several dances now, and was enjoying the event.

After stopping to greet the stage-line owner, Robinson had been engaged in conversation by the daughters, though that conversation kept coming back to his acquaintance with Jonah.

'You say his father is a doctor?' Opal asked, her green eyes wide. 'Why that's just too too wonderful! Isn't that a gentlemanly profession, Mama?'

'Young Mr. Durrell is not a doctor,' Mrs. Millard said. 'A bounty hunter is hardly the kind of man who would be well received in good society.'

'I beg your pardon, but Jonah Durrell has excellent manners and is worthy of anyone's society.' Robinson turned to face Mrs. Millard as he defended his friend. As he spoke, a piece of jewelry she wore caught his eye. Robinson paused, and the band leader announced the next dance. Thinking fast, Robinson offered his arm to Mrs. Millard. 'I would be delighted if you would honour me with the next dance.'

Mrs. Millard blinked, then smiled kindly. 'That would be welcome, thank you.'

Robinson led her onto the dancefloor; they joined a set and according to the called instructions, turned to face one another. As he bowed to her, Robinson took the opportunity to study the gold bar brooch pinned to the front of her gown. It had two small garnets set into it, and he was close enough now to see that the centre was engraved with a picture of mountains.

With his thoughts occupied by the brooch, Robinson almost missed the cue to begin dancing. Mrs. Millard took charge, grasping his hands to whisk him across the set. The dancing was too active to allow for chatter, but Robinson did manage to plan his next move as he carefully steered Mrs. Millard about the floor. When the dance finished, he escorted her back to her husband, and escaped before the girls could corner him to ask about Jonah again.

Robinson managed to catch the manhunter at the bar and urged him to step outside for a breath of fresh air. Jonah raised an eyebrow, then followed his friend.

'I'm hoping that you have a plumb good reason for wanting to come outside while there's still dancing going on,' Jonah said, once they were outside.

Robinson nodded earnestly. 'Have you made acquaintance with the Millards this evening?'

'I danced with both the daughters,' Jonah replied. 'The older one is given to baby talk, and the second one was sweet to me but sounded like she was raised on sour milk when she talked about her sister. Why, do you want advice on courting them?' He grinned wryly.

Robinson shook his head. 'Mrs. Millard is wearing a brooch just like the one Miss Louise had that was stolen by the bandits.'

115

The humour dropped from Jonah's face. 'You're sure?'

Robinson fished out his notebook and flipped through it. 'I wrote down her description of it, yeah? A gold bar brooch with a garnet at either end, and mountains engraved between.'

'It could be a coincidence,' Jonah said carefully. 'There must have been more than one made like that.'

Robinson nodded. 'Do we know where Miss Louise got her brooch?'

'She said it was given to her by a gentleman she knew in Independence, Kansas. The jewelry store in Silverton told me they'd had nothing that matched the description I gave. Have the Millards operated in or near Independence?'

Robinson consulted his notebook again. 'No. They came from Pennsylvania originally. Millard set up his first stage-line in Springfield, Missouri. A few years later he moved to Denver, then Boulder, then Cañon City for two years before settling here.'

'Settling is not what they seem to do,' Jonah remarked dryly. 'We need to find out when she got it; if it was before the stagecoach robbery, then it is just a coincidence.'

'You need to talk to her,' Robinson said. 'Ask her to waltz and then charm her so she answers your questions and doesn't even recall what you talked about, but only has the memory of your smile.'

'Are you my pimp now?' Jonah asked, half-indignant. 'Exploiting my looks for gain? There's more to me than being damned good-looking,' he added with some feeling.

'Of course there is,' Robinson said sincerely. 'But it's for a good cause, to which you have already applied intelligence and courage, yeah? And you're much better at charming women than I am so you'll get the task done more efficiently.'

Jonah relaxed a little and smiled. 'I'm sorry. I didn't mean to . . .' He gestured vaguely by way of explanation, then dismissed the subject. 'I'll go sacrifice my self-worth to the necessity of getting information from Mrs. Millard.'

'Good. I'll sacrifice my toes to the feet of Miss Pearl in case she can offer more information about the family as we dance.'

'Miss Opal's older; she might know more.'

Robinson shuddered. 'As a newspaperman, I pride myself on the correct and clear use of the English language. It hurts my soul to hear Miss Opal speak of this "too-too exciting lickle dance".' He mimicked her baby talk in a high-pitched voice.

Jonah laughed outright. 'I'll tell Jenny to have her girls only ever speak like that to you.' And dodged aside as Robinson tried to thump him on the shoulder.

CHAPTER TEN

Late the following morning, the two men met with Miss Jenny in her office.

'Her brooch was exactly like Louise's?' she queried, looking from one to the other.

'I must admit that although I saw Miss Louise wearing her brooch, I didn't pay too much attention to it,' Robinson said. 'Therefore, I cannot swear to the exact likeness, but Mrs. Millard's brooch, which I did observe with care, matched the description that Miss Louise gave of hers, yeah?'

'Mrs. Millard told me that her husband gave her her brooch four days ago,' Jonah said.

'That would be when he last came here,' Jenny said immediately. 'The bribe she extracts for allowing him to indulge his pleasures elsewhere.'

'So, she definitely got her brooch after the robbery,' Jonah said, thinking aloud. 'I asked in the jeweler's shop in Silverton, and they hadn't sold anything similar in the last few months, certainly not since the Millards arrived in the area. So, he didn't buy it locally.'

'Could Millard have gone to Durango or Denver to buy it?' Robinson asked.

Jenny shook her head. 'I don't think so. He's been coming here pretty regularly, almost since they arrived. I don't think he's been away long enough to travel as far as Durango or Montrose, let alone Denver.'

'It seems Millard can't have bought the brooch since moving to Motherlode. He could have purchased it before they relocated and simply not given it to his wife until now, but that does seem unlikely, as it was not given for a special occasion, like a birthday,' Robinson said. 'It appears he acquired a brooch just like Louise's recently, but not from a store.'

'It could have been a private trade: he took it in payment for a debt, maybe?' Jenny said doubtfully.

'That's possible,' Jonah agreed. 'But it's also possible that it is Louise's brooch, stolen during the stage robbery. The robbery's main target was the payroll and you're sure that the robbers knew it was there, aren't you?' he asked Robinson.

'As sure as I'm sitting here,' the newspaperman replied.

'The only people who knew the payroll would be

on that stage were the bank, the mine and the stage company,' Jonah said. 'We never found any sign of anyone from the mine who might have been involved. Millard owns the stage company and he's recently gotten hold of a brooch just like one that was stolen in the robbery. What's more, someone in this town wants me to stop looking into the robbery, and hired Russian Peter to put a scare into me,' he added with some feeling.

'Well, Millard didn't hold up the stage himself, so if he's involved, he must have tipped off the robbers,' Jenny said.

Robinson turned to Jonah. 'You identified two of the outlaws, didn't you?'

'Sure.' Jonah produced the two wanted notices from the pocket of his frock coat and handed them over. 'Here you are.'

After studying them for a minute, Robinson took out his notebook and flipped through it. His bony face was transformed with a smile as he read the squiggles of shorthand. 'I thought so.' He jabbed a finger at one of the notices. 'Both men were involved in a stage robbery near Boulder in '71. Millard was operating his stage line out of Boulder back then.'

'Was it his stage that was robbed?' Jenny asked eagerly, leaning to see the notice.

'That information isn't supplied, though I can check it,' Robinson admitted. 'But it does seem a coincidence, yeah? I thought it a little odd that they seemed to move so often; it surely doesn't make sense to get a business running, and then move to a new city a couple of years later and start over again.'

'People do that if their business is failing,' Jenny pointed out.

'But the Millards aren't struggling,' Robinson pointed out. 'Look at all the jewelry they wear. And it's a complete set up for the stagecoach business he has, with a carpenter shop and harness shop for repairs, and a . . . oh!' he exclaimed. 'There was a large man working in the yard when I went to interview Millard. I remember his face and the way he looked at me. I think he was Russian Peter, yeah?' He was talking faster and more excitedly. 'All the moves make sense if Millard is arranging for his stages to be robbed. He pulls it off two or three times in one location, then moves somewhere else and does it again there, then moves again before anyone sees a pattern forming.'

'Two payroll attacks over a couple of years wouldn't look too suspicious,' Jonah agreed. 'But if it happened more often, or kept happening to the same line, folks might start to wondering.'

'At the very least, they'd think the line was unlucky, and stop using it,' Jenny said.

'This is outside of Marshal Tapton's jurisdiction,

I believe,' Robinson said, looking at Jonah for con-
firmation. 'Should we inform the local sheriff of
our suspicions?'

Jonah shook his head. 'That's all we got, suspicions. There's a mighty lot of coincidences here –
the brooch, Russian Peter, those outlaws attacking
stage lines twice,' he said, gesturing at the wanted
posters. 'And we don't even know for sure if it was
Millard's line they attacked in Boulder. But it's all
circumstantial.'

Robinson flopped back untidily in his chair.
'You're correct,' he admitted.

They sat in silence for a few moments. Jenny
fiddled with her shawl; Jonah frowned and flexed
his fingers. Robinson lifted a hand and inspected
his fingernails.

'Our theory only works if Millard and the
outlaws are working together,' Robinson said
slowly, still staring at his nails as he thought. 'We
need a way of showing that Millard is passing information to them, yeah?' He absently began chewing
on a hangnail.

Jonah watched him with a pained expression. 'It
can't be another payroll robbery. The bank and the
mine will know when the next payroll's due, so that's
two other possible sources for the outlaws' information. It doesn't narrow it down to Millard.' He
extracted a small pair of folding scissors from a
pocket, opened them and passed them to Robinson.

Robinson studied him a moment, took one more nibble on the hangnail, then picked up the scissors to tackle it: Jonah relaxed. Jenny hid a smile, and resisted the temptation to start chewing on one of her own nails. Looking at her hands, the simple garnet ring she wore gave her an idea.

'We need a bait that will lure Millard specifically, and something he's greedy for.' Jenny smiled. 'Jewels.'

The men looked at one another.

'He's sure got a thing about jewels,' Jonah agreed.

'Do we have a quantity of jewels to be the bait?' Robinson asked.

'We don't need a casket of jewels,' Jenny pointed out. 'He just has to believe that there is one on his stagecoach. When the outlaws attack, all they find is people armed and waiting.'

'Who's going to be having the imaginary jewels delivered?' Robinson asked.

'I've never seen either of you two wearing much jewelry,' Jenny remarked. 'So, it had better be me. Some jewels that I left in the bank in Denver, that I'm having sent out now I'm settled here. One of the girls, probably Sandy, can let this slip to him when she's entertaining him on his next visit. If the outlaws attack, we know they were tipped off by Millard.'

'That sounds like it could work,' Jonah said

thoughtfully. 'But you could be putting yourself at some risk, if you're on the stage. You haven't actually lost anything to Millard, and Louise said she's not interested in revenge. I don't think you should take the risk.'

Jenny gave him a dark look. 'You don't get to tell me what I can and can't do. If we're right about what Millard's been doing, he's a scumbag, low-down criminal, and he needs to be stopped, along with the outlaws he's had working for him. I don't want crime happening here any more than any other citizen does. You know I've been in a fire-fight before, and that I know what I'm getting myself into. You two can't tackle half a dozen outlaws on your own; you're going to need someone else who can handle a gun, just as you did when we went to rescue Sandy. I'm going to be on that stage, escorting my jewels, with at least one of my girls. I'll ask Erica. It will be entirely voluntary, but I think she'll agree.'

Robinson looked at Jonah. 'She makes a good point.'

Jonah sighed. 'I guess I can't stop you, but I've said my piece.' He smiled. 'I can't think of a man I'd rather have along when it gets tough.'

Robinson raised an eyebrow. 'I feel vaguely insulted.'

Jonah laughed. 'All right, let's get to planning this.'

Millard was a little disappointed when he came home the following evening, and Mary wasn't in the hall to greet him. He guessed that she was in the kitchen, overseeing the cook's work, and headed for the parlour. His daughters were all there, as beautiful as ever in their lovely dresses with the lamplight glittering from their jewels. Amethyst promptly dropped her book and raced over to greet him, uninhibited by her mother's presence. Millard stooped and picked her up, whirling her around in delighted giggles. As he put her down again, he noticed that Opal and Pearl were arguing.

'I don't see why you should care that he's gone,' Pearl was saying. 'He only danced with you once. I danced with him twice.'

'I don't care, so there,' Opal retorted, tossing her hair. 'I'm going to Denver soon with Mamma and I'll find a better husband than Jonah Durrell.'

'You won't find a more handsome one.'

'Neither will you, especially now he's gone to Telluride. . . .'

'Now, girls. Don't argue, and over men. You know your mother wouldn't like it. She'd say it's common,' Millard interrupted.

Opal immediately collected herself and smiled sweetly at her father: Pearl stuck her tongue out quickly at her sister before turning and sitting down. Opal came and kissed Millard on the cheek by way of greeting.

'Thank you for letting me go to Denver, Papa,' she said breathlessly. 'It's just too-too exciting. I'm in a mad whirl about it all. There's so much to get ready!'

'That's all right, my dear,' Millard said. 'I'm sure your mother will cope splendidly.'

Opal moved to sit opposite Pearl, giving her sister a triumphant look that was missed by Millard as he had crossed to speak to Ruby, sitting at the table. She looked up from her history book with a smile.

'Still studying?' Millard asked. 'You should take a break.'

'Oh, Papa, I do want go to school,' she beseeched. 'It's so hard to keep up with lessons when we keep moving, and this town doesn't even have a school yet.'

'You can read and write and figure, and I'm sure you know as much history as I do,' Millard told her, putting his hand on her shoulder. 'You don't need a fancy education to catch a husband and you won't need it when you're married.'

'But, Papa.' Ruby pouted. 'I want to learn. Besides,' she added, changing tactics slightly, 'a successful businessman might not want a wife who doesn't know anything about anything except the latest styles. Some rich people like salons, where they speak French and talk about books. Don't you think I'd be better suited to that kind of a husband?'

Millard reflected while Ruby continued to gaze hopefully at him with blue eyes, so like her mother's.

'Going to boarding school would be a big step,' he mused. 'You'd be away from home for months at a time.'

'Yes!' Ruby just managed to moderate her reply so it didn't sound too enthusiastic. 'Please, Papa. If I'm at school, Mama can spend more of her time fixing up Opal and Pearl without needing to concern herself with me. Once they are married, I will have grown up some, and it will be my turn.' She smiled sweetly and did her best to look keen about her future marriage.

Millard gently brushed his hand across her head. 'I'll speak to your mother,' he promised. 'Now put your books away; it's almost time for dinner.'

The look of genuine gratitude went straight to his heart. Dear Ruby didn't really ask for much and he wanted to be able to give her something she so clearly longed for. Sending her to a decent school would be another expense though, on top of sending Opal to Denver. Business had gone well so far in Motherlode but with his daughters growing up, he seemed to be juggling money as much as ever. He wanted to have a nice, sound nest-egg for his retirement by the time little Amethyst left home, and there would be grandchildren to provide for in the future. Millard settled in his favourite armchair and watched Opal at her tatting while daydreaming about his future grandchildren.

CHAPTER ELEVEN

'Well, I've had a nice day out,' Erica said. 'It's nice to see another town and look at some different shops.'

Robinson, sitting opposite her and beside Jenny inside the stagecoach on the trail back from Silverton to Motherlode, looked at her curiously. Erica smiled back, eyes amused.

'Nothing may happen, in which case it's been a nice day,' she said. 'If the bandits do attack and people get hurt, well it's in a good cause and at least we've had the pleasure of the outing beforehand.'

When planning the trap for Millard's outlaws, there had been some discussion about who should travel where. Obviously, Jenny and Erica would travel in the stage, with the imaginary jewels. Robinson had travelled to Silverton the day before, rather than in the morning with the women, so he wouldn't necessarily be expected to return with them. Jonah had returned to Silverton from Telluride late the night before and had stayed out of sight. He preferred the flexibility of horseback travel to joining the others in the stage, but had hired a brown, instead of his distinctive grey, and changed his usual hat for a lower, wide-brimmed one. He was riding close behind the stagecoach, where he would be harder for the outlaws to see from their likely ambush positions.

'If Millard is behind these robberies, I bet it's his wife who has been encouraging him,' Jenny commented. 'She's got ambition written all over her.'

'She may think Lady Macbeth is an inspiring example, yeah?' Robinson suggested.

Erica chuckled. 'If you mentioned Lady Macbeth to her, she'd probably assume she was one of Queen Victoria's ladies-in-waiting.'

The laughter lightened the mood. Conversation continued for a while, but as the stage got closer to the site of the previous attack, the people waiting inside became quiet. Robinson was the first to pick up a weapon, checking over his borrowed shotgun, then settling it with the muzzle carefully pointed towards the door. The women shortly followed his example. The strained silence lasted a couple of minutes.

'I shall feel an awful fool if nothing happens,' Erica said, with a tight smile.

'There's no one but us to see, and we're doing

the same thing, yeah?' Robinson said. 'If we reach. . . .'

The gunshot made them all jump. It was followed by a shout demanding that the stagecoach halt. The three passengers braced themselves as the swaying coach lurched to a stop. Jenny and Robinson unlatched the doors, but held them closed while looking out. Pairs of armed bandits were now approaching the stage on foot from either side, while a fifth man held the horses.

'Now!' Jonah's command from behind the stage, was quiet but firm.

Robinson and Jenny flung their doors open and jumped out. Jenny stayed behind her door, using the small amount of shelter it provided as she brought her rifle smoothly to her shoulder, aiming through the glassless window. Jonah ran out from behind the coach to support her, the matched Smith and Wessons in hand. On the other side, Robinson landed awkwardly and lurched forward, trying to catch his balance and aim his shotgun at the same time. Behind him, Erica swung out neatly and took up the same position as Jenny.

'Surrender!' shouted Jonah. 'Throw down your weapons!'

There was a moment's confusion among the outlaws. Of the two facing Robinson, one glanced across to the other group, seeking guidance; the second lifted his gun, unsure which target to aim at.

'Get the men!' yelled the leader, aiming for Jonah.

Blasts of gunfire erupted in the quiet valley. Robinson instinctively went for the outlaw who was raising his gun. The man jerked once, screaming, then again as Erica's shot hit him. Blood sprayed from the two shotgun wounds as he collapsed. Robinson froze momentarily, gaping at the moaning, torn figure on the ground. He'd seen shootings before, and as he'd told Jonah, he'd fought Comanches some ten years earlier, but this was the first time he'd shot a white man himself. Killing a man who looked and dressed like himself, and who spoke the same language, was not the same as killing an unknowable outsider like a Comanche.

As he hesitated, the second man turned and fled. The sudden movement jerked Robinson back to the present. He stepped sideways to get a better angle, changing the aim of his shotgun. As his mind began to catch up with the action again, he abruptly realized his mistake, even as he heard fluent cursing from behind, delivered in the most cut-glass English accent. Robinson hurriedly returned to his previous place, clearing Erica's line of sight to the fleeing man. By this time, the outlaw was level with the lead horses and too close to them to risk a shot. Erica emerged from behind the stagecoach door, glaring at Robinson and using language completely at odds with her lady-like tones.

On the other side of the stagecoach, Jonah fired both handguns. He missed the outlaw leader, who ducked aside after yelling for his men to attack. He couldn't tell if his other shot hit, as Jenny fired at the second outlaw at the same time. The short man screamed, staggering back as he tried to stay on his feet. The leader fired, hitting nothing so far as Jonah could tell.

'Surrender!' Jonah yelled again. He stepped sideways while bringing both guns to bear on the leader.

He saw the man's eyes focus above the bandanna mask, knew he was going to shoot, and twisted aside, shooting as he moved. The leader fired back as he flung himself to the ground. There was a sudden confusion of shots: handguns and Jenny's rifle. There was a yell of pain from someone he couldn't see, and a sudden exclamation from Jenny that made his heart race. The injured outlaw was yelling and cursing as he let off shots towards the stage. Jonah fired one gun at him, noticing that the leader was scrambling to his feet but turning away. Ducking back and forth, Jonah fired a couple more shots to cover himself as he glanced in Jenny's direction.

She was still behind the open door of the stage and apparently unharmed, as she was aiming her rifle through the open window again. As Jonah turned his attention back to the bandits, she fired, this time sending the injured man to the ground. The leader had made his feet and was running to the man with the horses, who was advancing to meet him. Jonah fired at the leader but was distracted by the stage guard, who was shrieking in pain. He wanted to catch the outlaws, but they were clearly retreating, and his conscience was urging him to tend to the guard who had been injured in a trap he hadn't known he'd been a part of. Making a quick decision, Jonah took a shot at the fleeing leader. He missed, but one of the horses shied as the bullet zipped past, almost pulling loose from the man holding the reins.

A third outlaw appeared from the other side of the stage horses. He fired a couple of shots at Jonah, as he ran to join the other two. Jonah weaved about, making himself a harder target, as the smell of black powder sharpened the air. He took one shot in return and heard the bark of Jenny's rifle. One of the outlaws' horses screamed and bucked. The outlaws were throwing themselves into their saddles, hanging on as their mounts danced about. The horse holder had released one of the spares and it galloped towards Jonah, its eyes wild. He dodged sideways to avoid it and collided with Jenny, who had moved out from the shelter of the stagecoach.

Both staggered as the horse thundered past. Jonah caught his balance and looked at Jenny.

'Are you all right?' he asked.

'Fine.' She spoke loudly to be heard over the shrieks of the injured guard and the pounding of hoofs as the outlaws fled. Her eyes were bright and she was breathing heavily, but otherwise she seemed to be composed in the aftermath of the fight.

'Good.' He flashed her a smile before turning his attention back to business.

The three surviving outlaws were racing away, heading towards Motherlode. Jonah approached the man Jenny had shot. The short outlaw was on the ground, moaning softly and shuddering, but Jonah remained cautious, glad that Jenny was close by with her rifle at the ready. As Jonah knelt to examine him more closely, there was a shout from the front of the stage.

'Hey! Leave that scum! Tom needs help urgent-like.'

Jonah looked up at the stage driver, who had the wailing guard slumped against him. He picked up the outlaw's dropped Colt and rose to hand it to Jenny, saying softly;

'Anyone making that much noise probably isn't hurt too bad.'

As he moved closer to the stage, Robinson came

around from the other side to join them.

'We shot one man, but the other desperado escaped, yeah?' he reported.

'Is Erica all right?' Jenny asked.

Robinson nodded. 'Oh, yes. She was most calm in the event of. . . .'

Jonah interrupted him. 'Give me a hand to get this man down so's I can tend to him.'

'Oh, certainly.' Enthusiasm was replaced with concern as Robinson paid attention to the still-wailing guard. Putting his shotgun down, he went to help.

The injured man was carefully helped down and laid beside the trail. He continued to moan and wail as Jonah pulled open his jacket and examined him. The clothes on the right-hand side of his chest were soaked with blood.

'Hold still,' Jonah ordered as he started cutting the sticky shirt open with his knife.

'I'm dying, I'm dying,' the guard moaned. 'My chest hurts so bad.' He turned his head towards Jenny. 'Oh, say a prayer for me, pretty lady. Oww!' He squawked as Jonah pressed against his chest.

Jonah inspected the wound again. 'Broken rib, I reckon. The lung's not punctured. The bullet grazed your side and glanced off the rib. A few stitches and some bandages and you'll feel much better. Be all fixed in a few weeks.'

The wounded guard glared at him. 'I'm hurt

bad! What in hell do you know about medicine, manhunter?'

'More than you do,' Jonah retorted, unperturbed. 'Now quit wailing like a baby; we've got work to do here and there's three sorry outlaws headed back to town we need to catch up with.'

Robinson and Jenny checked on the injured outlaw. He was unconscious, his breathing shallow and irregular.

'I doubt if there's any practical way of aiding him now,' Robinson said. He studied the short man for a few moments, then pulled down the bandanna that still concealed his features. 'I do believe this is the one who attacked Miss Louise; Brewster, his name is.'

'I didn't feel that bad for shooting him,' Jenny said. 'And less so now. He's the kind that thinks he has the right to do what he wants with a woman and he likes to brag on it too. I bet Louise isn't the only one he's raped.'

'We should at least make him comfortable in his last moments, yeah?' Robinson said. He used Brewster's own bandanna to wipe blood from the man's mouth. 'Taking a person's life is a serious business,' he mused. 'He chose to commit dreadful crimes, and he would have shot any of us to protect himself, but when you see someone dying in front of you, from your bullets, I can't help wondering if I had the right to take that life away.' He glanced over at Jonah. 'This experience will make an excellent topic for my letters to the *New-York Tribune* about Jonah. I must ask him. . . .'

His flow of thought was interrupted by Erica, appearing from the other side of the stage. She hurried towards them with a triumphant expression.

'He confessed!' she announced. 'The man we shot. He was barely conscious, but he was cursing and blaming someone for betraying them. I asked who it was and he said Millard. Millard paid them to rob his stagecoaches.'

'That's excellent news,' beamed Robinson.

'Is he still alive?' Jenny asked urgently.

Erica shook her head. 'He died a few moments ago.'

'Damn.' Jenny looked at the others. 'The confession's worthless then. There was only one witness and remember what Marshal Tapton said when we brought those thieves in? No jury's going to take a woman's word over a man's, especially if she's a prostitute. Millard will simply deny everything.'

Erica's face fell. 'You're right. Nothing would happen to him and I'd be humiliated. It's so unfair!' she burst out. 'We risked our lives to set this up, and that poor guard got injured. We know Millard is responsible for the thefts, but we still have no way of adequately proving it. We're no better off than we were before.'

There was a short silence after her emphatic statement.

'We've accomplished one thing,' Jenny said. She indicated the dying outlaw. 'That's the piece of scum who raped Louise. He'll never hurt anyone else.'

There was another silence, broken by a call from Jonah.

'I need some help here. I need warm water to wash this wound before I stitch it. We should get ready to move on when I'm done fixing things up here.'

Robinson stood up, gradually unfolding his ungainly length. 'We should reload our guns and stay alert. The bandits could come back, yeah?'

'They'll regret it if they do,' Erica said simply.

Millard looked up as the door to his office burst open, banging against the wall. Kellner barged in, followed by two of his men. They were dusty from the trail, and empty-handed. Millard rose swiftly as the outlaws strode up to his desk.

'Where are the jewels?' he demanded.

'We didn't get them, if there were any,' Kellner spat back. 'It was a set up. I lost two of my men back there.'

'The law?' Millard asked. 'Have you led the law straight here?' He glowered at the outlaws. All trace of the genial gnome was gone and his broad frame and balding head looked simply thuggish.

Kellner shook his head. 'It was that damned manhunter, the tall madam and one of her whores and some feller as tall as all get out. He was on the stage when we first robbed it.'

Millard looked shocked. 'Robinson? He's a newspaperman. He was going to write a letter about me for the *New-York Tribune*.' He felt a pang of disappointment: that letter would surely never appear now. Then he recalled something else. 'Robinson told me that Durrell had gone to Telluride. He lied to me – they must have set Madam Jenny up as bait in their trap.'

'Those whores were in on it,' Kellner asserted. 'They were both armed and it was that madam that put Brewster down.'

Millard scowled more than ever. 'I wouldn't have believed it,' he growled. 'Those ungrateful bitches. I treated them like they were decent women, and this is how they repay me. I bet they dragged Durrell and. . . .'

'We want money.' Kellner interrupted Millard's musing. He leaned over the desk, pushing his face close to the businessman's. 'You owe us.'

Millard stared right back, refusing to be intimidated. 'You didn't do your job properly.'

'We ambushed the stage like you told us to. It ain't our fault there probably weren't any jewels on there.'

Millard inwardly admitted that the outlaw was likely right: the promised jewels had been invented as a trap for him, and he'd fallen into it. He didn't let any doubt show though, just his anger at being taken for a ride. 'Did you kill them?' he growled.

Kellner shook his head, looking sheepish briefly before glaring again. 'No. And we're through here. It's too risky to keep working this area with a manhunter like Durrell after us. Give us our money so we can hit the trail, or you'll be the one on the wrong end of a bullet.'

'No!' Millard snapped. 'They've figured out our scheme. You have to kill the men and silence the women. No . . .' He hesitated a moment. 'They have to die too. I can't take the risk, and besides, they just showed their true nature as abominations against the good name of "woman". I can't count them as women any longer.'

'There ain't but three of us and there's four of them, plus the stage driver and guard. And we're not going anywhere without some gold.' Kellner's hand dropped towards his gun.

Millard made some fast calculations, weighing the value of the outlaws against the money in his safe. 'All right. There's not much in the safe here but I'll give you something now. Once Durrell and the others are dead, I'll get more from the bank and pay you.'

'The three of us still won't be enough. If we ride,

you're coming with us.'

'I'm not. . . .'

'There's more of us than you!' Kellner drew his gun, his men following suit. 'Iffen you want to better the odds, get more men along with us. Your stage guards, anyone who can hold a gun and point it in the right direction.'

Millard took a deep breath, glowering at the outlaws. 'Russian Peter's around. He can find some others.'

'Good.' Kellner nodded. 'Now open that safe and give us some money.'

Millard turned to the safe, resentful of the actions he'd been forced into. He wasn't sure what hurt most: being let down by Kellner, or being betrayed by Jenny. Somehow, it was the betrayal by a woman that seemed to hurt most.

CHAPTER TWELVE

Robinson's height came in very useful for helping to load the bodies of the dead outlaws on top of the stagecoach. Brewster, the one who had raped Louise, had died while Jonah was still tending to the guard. Robinson was heaving the one he and Erica had killed, up to the driver, trying not to rock the stage too much, as Jonah was inside, making the injured guard as comfortable as possible in the confined space. On the other side of the stage, Jenny heard something moving further along the trail, in the direction of Motherlode. Nothing was immediately visible, as the trail curved past an outcrop of trees that the bandits had used for cover. She got Erica's attention, and picked up her rifle.

Two horsemen came into view, moving at a steady jog. Neither had a weapon in hand, so she waited a few moments until she could see them more clearly.

'Why, it's Millard!' she exclaimed, relaxing a little.

Millard waved as he approached. 'I got worried when the stage was late,' he called.

'But isn't he the one we thought organized the ambush?' Erica said quietly to Jenny.

Jenny turned to Erica, and in that moment Millard waved his arm in a signal.

The three outlaws burst out from the trees, guns in hand. Two of them immediately fired at the women near the stage. Erica flung herself flat, wriggling forward slightly to take advantage of a shallow depression that offered some cover. Jenny snugged her rifle to her shoulder and aimed. It was longish range for pistols and the men were firing from galloping horses: she gambled on them missing her while she took one good shot. Her finger was tightening on the trigger when the third outlaw fired. Jenny felt something tear through her skirt. Her aim wavered at the moment she fired. Without waiting to see if she'd hit, Jenny dropped to the ground alongside Erica.

Jonah hadn't paid too much attention to the sounds from outside, being occupied with the injured guard. After learning that Jonah had had medical training, the guard had begun describing symptoms that could have indicated a kidney stone, or which could have been hypochondria.

144

The guard was describing the throbbing pain in his side, when the first shots were fired. Jonah immediately jumped to his feet and headed to the door, automatically identifying the type of guns from the sound, and their distance, even before he could see anything.

'Don't leave me alone!' The guard grabbed Jonah's wrist. 'I'm unarmed.'

Caught off-balance, it took Jonah a few moments to be able to pull himself free. His eyes flashed with anger, but he didn't waste breath on curses. Instead he threw open the door and jumped out. He saw Jenny and Erica lying out in the open, armed, with three horsemen charging towards them. Even as he was drawing his revolvers, he glimpsed another horseman much closer, approaching from his left. Glancing that way, Jonah noted another rider further back, watching, and that the closest rider was not holding a gun. Ignoring him for the moment, Jonah raised one gun and took a moment to aim.

He'd just got one of the three riders in his sights when he felt a sudden sense of dread about the approaching rider on his left. Jonah took a deep breath, swallowing his fear as he fought to concentrate on his shot. He fired, saw his target jerk, and turned to face the nearer rider. The burly man was throwing himself off his horse as it came to an earth-tearing halt. It was Russian Peter. A cold shudder ran up Jonah's spine as he saw Russian Peter drawing his knife. Acting on pure instinct, he pointed and shot. The hammer clicked on an empty chamber. Occupied by the injured guard, Jonah had forgotten to reload.

For once, Jonah simply panicked. He pulled the trigger twice more, with the same result. Russian Peter advanced slowly, weaving the knife about at head height as he smiled coldly. Jonah's hand twitched, as though to throw the useless gun aside, but he couldn't relinquish the weapon. Russian Peter was just a few feet away now, the slowly-moving knife drawing Jonah's gaze as though mesmerized.

'Good Lord. Look out!'

Robinson's voice jerked Jonah back to reality. Russian Peter saw the change and attacked.

When he'd heard the shots, Robinson had simply given one last shove to the outlaw's corpse and run, picking up his shotgun as he headed around the back of the stagecoach to see what was happening. His shout was directed at Jonah, but his attention was immediately drawn to the three riders galloping towards Jenny and Erica, who were lying in their path. Without thinking about what he was doing, Robinson yelled to attract the outlaws' attention.

Throwing his shotgun to his shoulder, he took a hasty shot at the one on the left. Jenny fired at almost the same moment. Their target reeled in his saddle, screaming, as his horse slowed and swerved. Jenny rolled over, away from Kellner, who was in the middle of the three outlaws. Her elaborate skirts hampered her movement, leaving her struggling on the ground.

Erica held her fire as she watched the third outlaw gallop towards her. Unlike the others, he was urging his horse faster, his swarthy face creased in a cruel grin. From where she was lying, it was difficult for her to shoot him without hurting his horse, which she was reluctant to do. He had his gun in hand, but wasn't yet aiming for her. Erica guessed at what he intended, and waited, pressed flat to the grass. It seemed as though she could feel the hard impact of the horse's hoofs through the ground as it closed on her. When it was just a stride away, Erica curled up her legs and tensed. Dust rose from the ground, the horse grunted and then its dark shaped passed over her as it jumped. The hind hoofs had barely cleared her head before Erica was twisting onto her back and sitting up in the same move. The outlaw may have wanted to trample her, but Erica had gambled correctly on the horse's reluctance to tread on an obstacle like a fallen human. As she brought the shotgun to her shoulder, the outlaw was hauling on his reins, trying to spin his horse. Erica had a clear shot at him and took it, sending a load of buckshot into his back.

Robinson saw Jenny struggling and ran closer. Kellner was reining in his horse: he glanced at the newspaperman holding his shotgun, then at the woman with her repeating rifle. Ignoring Robinson, he took aim at Jenny. Robinson yelled and fired off a quick shot. Kellner flinched, stung by some of the buckshot. Fiercely controlling his frightened horse, he changed aim. Robinson was about to fire again, then realized that he'd emptied both barrels of the shotgun. He frantically twisted aside as Kellner fired. Something seemed to punch him high in the chest and he staggered back, his left arm falling to his side. Kellner pulled back the hammer for another shot.

Russian Peter darted forward, slashing the knife at Jonah's face. Jonah went to block the move with his empty gun and saw the look of triumph in Russian Peter's slate-blue eyes just a moment too late. The Russian grabbed Jonah's other hand and twisted it painfully, nearly making him drop his other pistol. His fingers were being crushed against the revolver, but Jonah couldn't spare the time to free himself from the powerful grip. Russian Peter sliced at him again with his knife. Fear shot up Jonah's spine like a jolt of electricity but this time he didn't panic. Instead, he was spurred to anger at his own weakness, his vanity.

Deflecting the knife with the revolver, Jonah quickly slammed the butt into Russian Peter's nose. The big man hissed a curse, crushing his hand tighter around Jonah's trapped hand. The knife came around again, lower this time. Jonah pulled hard with his left hand, twisting his body. He managed to pull the Russian's left arm between his ribs and the knife, forcing him to pull short the attack. Having to suddenly stop his move also threw Russian Peter slightly off balance. Jonah felt the change in weight and acted immediately.

He slammed his body into his opponent. As Russian Peter rocked back, Jonah hooked his foot behind the other man's leg. The Russian was flailing with his free hand, trying to keep his balance. Jonah shoved hard with his trapped hand and simultaneously smashed Peter in the face with his gun again. The Russian cried out as he fell backwards, blood springing from his mashed lips. He towed Jonah with him as he went, still clutching the hand he controlled. Russian Peter managed to push Jonah as they fell, so the manhunter landed partly on the ground beside him.

Jonah mostly broke his fall with his right arm. Changing tactics, he let go of the empty pistol. From the corner of his eye, he could see Russian Peter lifting the knife for another attack. Bracing himself with right hand and knee, Jonah twisted, and rammed his left knee into the other man's crotch. He couldn't get much force into the blow, but it was enough to distract Peter for a few, vital

149

moments. It was long enough for Jonah to reach across with his right hand and take the other gun from his trapped left hand. Grimacing with effort, Russian Peter crushed harder on Jonah's now-empty hand as he pinned Jonah's leg beneath his own and raised the knife again. Jonah spun the Smith and Wesson around in his right hand, the familiar shape of the gun nestling into his palm. His fingers instinctively found the right places even though he could hardly see what he was doing as he lay tangled with the Russian. He glimpsed sunlight flashing on the blade as the knife plunged towards his ribs. Jonah thumbed the hammer and pulled the trigger in a split second.

The explosion so close to his ear deafened him. Jonah flinched, his left hand pulling free from Russian Peter's suddenly limp grip. Something struck his side heavily: Peter's other arm with the knife dropping harmlessly beside it. Jonah lay still for a moment, trying to locate other sources of pain besides his throbbing, crushed fingers and his ringing ear. The air smelt of sweat, gunpowder and blood. Just a few inches from his face were the gory remains of Russian Peter's head, the eyes staring emptily at the sky above. Jonah felt giddily alive and triumphant, realizing he'd defeated his fear. Sucking in a deep breath, Jonah began to wriggle clear, looking about to see what else was happening.

Robinson burst into a zigzag sprint, getting stabs of pain from his shoulder with every step. He had no plan other than to somehow help Jenny. He saw Kellner fire a quick shot but felt nothing. As Kellner tried to correct his aim, Robinson flung himself in the opposite direction, long limbs flailing untidily. Kellner tracked him, eyes narrowing as he concentrated. Jenny, given a few moments to aim, fired. Her shot took Kellner through the upper chest. He stayed still for a moment, before buckling and starting to slide from his saddle.

The outlaw grabbed for his saddle horn with his free hand, struggling to bring his gun up again. Jenny took no chances but shot again. Kellner dropped his gun and toppled from his saddle, hanging with his feet tangled in the stirrups. Robinson thankfully came to a halt and looked around. To his relief, Erica was scrambling to her feet. Her shotgun was trained on the body of the outlaw who'd charged at her. He lay on the ground beside his snorting, shuddering horse. To Robinson's other side, the outlaw he and Jenny had shot was still in his saddle. He was hanging onto the mane of his horse as it sidled about, its ears flickering back and forth. Jenny too was rising, her rifle in one hand as she pulled her skirts out of the way.

'Don't ... don't shoot,' the outlaw begged. Patches of blood blossomed across his clothes. He

151

looked from Jenny to Robinson, his eyes pleading and distressed.

A single shot cracked in the quiet. The wounded man made a gargling sound and folded over, reluctantly sliding to the ground.

'Millard!'

The businessman was riding up, gun in hand. 'He was going to shoot!'

'He was surrendering!' Jenny protested.

Robinson and Jenny both reached the fallen man. As they knelt down, they heard indistinct sounds of pain between the spasmodic breaths. Robinson ducked his head close, putting his good hand on the dying man's shoulder. He stayed like that for long seconds until the irregular breathing ceased.

'Explain yourself, Millard.' The order came from Jonah, who was back on his feet and had his gun pointed at the businessman.

Millard lowered his own gun. 'They forced me into it all,' he said anxiously. 'Kellner came to me just after we moved here. He said I had to tell him when we were carrying payrolls, or else he'd hurt my family.' The words tumbled out fast. 'They burst into my office and forced me to come along with them. They wanted revenge on you.'

'It's quite a coincidence that Kellner should come to you here in Motherlode, yeah?' Robinson rose slowly to his feet, cradling his damaged arm with the other one. 'He's been making quite a habit of robbing your stagecoaches over the last few years.'

Millard looked hurt. 'I don't know what you mean.'

Robinson approached him. 'I got curious about why you'd moved your business so often. I wrote the editors of newspapers in Cañon City, Boulder and Denver.' He paused as he fished awkwardly in his left jacket pocket with his right hand. 'I got more replies today while I was in Silverton.' He successfully extracted a couple of envelopes and held them up. Millard went white but held his silence. 'I don't believe anyone put these reports together before,' Robinson went on. 'You kept moving from town to town and changing the name of your companies. But in every location, you had big payrolls stolen from your stages – only a couple from each line, but they were all considerable sums of money. Kellner and his ruffians were implicated in every one of those robberies. And moreover, we have a confession: that man's dying words.' He waved the envelopes in the direction of Jenny and the dead outlaw. 'He said it was your idea, Millard.'

Millard stared at Robinson, his face stricken. He missed Jenny's brief look of surprise, as she had heard no confession from the dying man.

'Drop the gun, Millard,' Jonah ordered, moving

closer. 'I'm taking you in for robbery and murder. Maybe your wife can wear the brooch you gave her, that was stolen from Miss Louise, when she attends your trial.'

Millard flushed with anger, then crumpled. 'Oh, Mary! I've let her down; she'll be furious.'

Jonah grinned humourlessly. 'Maybe it's just as well you won't be going home tonight.'

Millard let the gun drop to the ground as he began sobbing. Jonah looked to the women.

'Just cover him while I get him cuffed, then I'll see to Robinson's arm and we can get home.'

The late arrival of the stage in Motherlode, with bodies strapped to the roof, and the line's owner in handcuffs, caused something of a sensation. Marshal Tapton grumbled from behind his moustache, but Jonah and Robinson persuaded him to put Millard in the cells and wire the county sheriff. With that done, Jonah promptly announced that he needed to fix Robinson's injury and hustled his friend away, leaving the marshal to take care of the bodies, the injured guard and the rest of the mess.

Back at the parlour house, Jonah stitched and bandaged the wound. A bullet had glanced off Robinson's collar-bone, breaking it and leaving a gash across the top of his shoulder. With the wound tended to, and a sling for his arm, the newspaperman declared himself to be comfortable.

Louise appeared from the kitchen, bearing a plate of fresh, hot vanity cakes.

'I don't reckon as how I'm very good at saying thank you,' she said, offering around the crisp, brown cakes. 'This seemed as good as anything.'

'How clever of you to bake something I can eat with one hand,' Robinson observed, taking one and biting into it.

'I do appreciate that you cared about what happened to me,' Louise continued, setting the plate on the table. 'That ain't happened much afore. It's . . . it's good to feel it.' She gave a quick nod and left without waiting for a reply.

Jonah looked at Jenny. 'You know I'm only too glad to help.'

'I do. Every woman in town should be grateful that Brewster and his friends are dead.'

A clock chimed and Jenny quickly glanced at it. 'Good heavens! I have to bathe and get ready for tonight. You're both welcome to stay and enjoy yourself with the compliments of the house this evening.'

Robinson brushed crumbs from his chin. 'I'm afraid my injury rather prohibits me from enjoying any sport with your ladies at the moment. As much as I enjoy their company, I'd rather like to get down my impressions of today's events while they're still fresh in my mind. My letters about the stagecoach business will have a most thrilling conclusion.'

Jenny nodded. 'I understand. Oh, yes. You lied when you told Millard that you heard a dying confession. I never heard anything.'

Jonah looked at Robinson in surprise. The newspaperman smiled.

'Well, yes; it was a partial untruth. Miss Erica swore that one of the others confessed of Millard's part in the robberies, remember? I believe her, but Millard would not, and neither would many other men. So, I claimed to have heard a confession in order to persuade Millard to surrender to us peacefully. I am willing to swear to it in a court of law if necessary.'

'It may not come to that,' Jonah said. He rose gracefully. 'I'll be glad to accept the invitation for this evening, but I want to go to the hotel to get washed up and change.'

Robinson struggled awkwardly to his feet and the two men made their farewells.

Business was very good at the parlour house that evening. Word had spread of the women's involvement in the stagecoach attack and Millard's arrest, and men wanted to find out more. With the relief at a troublesome gang of outlaws being dealt with, a party atmosphere soon developed. Takings at the bar were excellent and all the girls had as much custom as they wanted. Jenny was busy all night, telling her version of events over and over, as well as with her usual work as hostess. By the time the last customer had left, several of her girls had already retired to bed and the rest followed soon after.

In the end, Jenny was left in the private parlour with Jonah, sipping at tea. She let her head rest against the back of her chair and smiled at him.

'I've hardly spoken to you all night. Did you have a good time?'

'Certainly,' he replied, his dark eyes on her face. 'It's good to feel that this is all over and we can rest for a while.'

'There's no need to ride out anywhere tomorrow,' Jenny agreed. 'Which may be as well,' she added, nodding towards the window.

Heavy rain was drumming on the glass and draughts around the frame made the curtains stir now and again.

'It's not a nice night to be out,' Jonah agreed.

Jenny finished her tea. 'There's no need for you to get soaked going back to your hotel. There's an empty room here you can sleep in.'

'Thank you.' Jonah stood up. Standing by her chair, he looked down at her and held out his hand. 'I'd really like it if you'd share it with me tonight?'

Jenny was taken aback by his question. Her relationships with men had always been centred around money: as prostitute, madam and business owner. Jonah was the only one who ever seemed to be interested in her for herself, as a friend. She looked at him, handsome and vital. A man who could charm any woman he chose and afford to pay for the best available. As she met his eyes, she saw anxiety. She was puzzled for a moment, then realized that this handsome, kind and generous man was worried in case she rejected him. She smiled.

'I will.'

She took his hand.